THE SYNDICATE SIX MURDER

A totally gripping whodunnit full of twists

GEOFFREY OSBORNE

JOFFE
BOOKS

First published 2020
Joffe Books, London
www.joffebooks.com

**Please join our mailing list for free
Kindle books and new releases.**

www.joffebooks.com

We love to hear from our readers! Please email any feedback you have to: feedback@joffebooks.com

ISBN 978-1-78931-556-1

AUTHOR'S NOTE

This book is dedicated to the late Chief Superintendent Clive Lewis, who was married to my wife's cousin Adrienne.

During his career with Kent Police Clive spent three years in the early 1980s seconded as a tutor at Bramshill, the world-famous Police Staff College in north-east Hampshire, and he invited me and my wife, Dorothy, to spend a weekend there.

The setting of the college in a large country estate, including a lake complete with Canada geese, was breathtaking. But it was the Jacobean mansion dominating the modern buildings on the campus that held the biggest surprise for me. In the magnificent entrance hall, where we had arranged to meet Clive and Adrienne, the first thing that gripped my attention was an old, ornate chest.

My shout that it was "just the right size for a body!" prompted Clive to say that it had once indeed held a body, and he went on to tell the legend of the seventeenth-century bride whose skeleton was found in the chest. Fascinated, I said I would write a present-day tale about the chest — and vowed that I would call it *The Syndicate Six Murder*, because courses at the college were numbered and called syndicates. And I knew Clive was in charge of Syndicate Six.

The day job, other books and short stories got in the way. But now, at last Clive, here it is . . . the book that would never have been written if you hadn't invited me to Bramshill all those years ago.

The Police Staff College closed in 2015 and the Home Office sold the site. Many of the posts mentioned in this story existed, and some still do. So, I must point out that all the characters are fictitious and bear no resemblance to any person, living or dead. Excepting the ghosts, of course.

They are real.

Are they looking for new homes, I wonder . . . ?

Geoffrey Osborne

CHAPTER ONE

THE ORNATELY carved, long wooden chest stood in a corner of the Jacobean mansion's grand entrance hall. As always, the lid was open, propped against the wall. Detective Superintendent Ralph Blade leaned forward to look inside.

The man in the chest was dead. There could be no doubt about that. And yet . . .

It was the eyes that seized Blade's attention. They seemed to recognise him, meeting his gaze with a cold stare, almost of hate. The man's lips were frozen in a rictus sneer of triumph, mocking him.

The hall spun. Blade, suddenly dizzy, felt his legs begin to buckle as alternating waves of darkness and light threatened to engulf him.

"Ralph, are you all right?"

Seeming to come from a distance, as if through a blanket of fog, the question jerked him back to consciousness. Realising that he'd been holding his breath, he took in a lungful of air. Instinctively, he avoided grabbing the chest for support. *Fingerprints . . . Crime scene . . . Don't contaminate.* He struggled upright and turned to face the speaker.

1

"I'm fine, Fred. Tired, that's all. I didn't get to bed until after one and it's still only," he glanced at his watch, "ten to six. And I haven't had breakfast," he added, cross.

"Well, you don't look fine, and you sound quite shaky. I think you should—"

Blade cut short Dr Stoker's suggestion. He drew himself up to his full six foot three and looked down at the pathologist, towering over the doctor's five foot six.

"I told you I'm all right. Okay?" He turned towards the chest, muttering something under his breath. "So, what have we got here?"

Despite the neatly trimmed grey hair and rimless spectacles, Stoker's smooth, round face displayed nothing of his sixty-three years, an illusion of youthfulness compounded by twinkling blue eyes and a willing smile. He was not smiling now. In saggy white overalls two sizes too big, and with his face mask dangling from one ear, he shifted uncomfortably on his feet.

He sighed. "SOCO and forensics are on their way. I haven't touched anything, apart from establishing that he's dead." He hesitated. "I may be wrong, but I thought I caught a whiff of bitter almonds. You didn't notice it?"

Blade shook his head. "Prussic acid? Cyanide? You think . . . ?"

"As I said, I may be wrong. You'll have to wait until I get him on the table."

Blade's brow creased pensively as his right forefinger and thumb slid down the sides of his cheeks, pausing under his chin to pinch the flesh. There seemed to be more to pinch now that he had turned forty, but his smart grey suit easily disguised the beginnings of a bulge around his middle. His closely cropped hair was turning grey too, but the bright blue of his eyes destroyed any sense of drabness.

He stroked his cheeks again, seemed about to speak, but changed his mind, turned and stalked across the hall to a uniformed policeman standing guard just inside the impressive wooden front door.

"What can you tell me, Constable?"

The young officer saluted. "We was in the area, sir, and we got a radio message that a body had been found here. When we arrived, there was four cleaning ladies standing where we are now, sir. In a right state they was, and they pointed to the chest and said there was a dead man in it. We went over and had a look. We could see straight away that they was right. He *was* dead. Nothing we could do."

"Did you touch anything?"

"No, sir. I called the station and they told us to stay here until—"

Blade made an impatient gesture. "Where are these ladies now?"

The constable pointed to a passage. "In a room through there. My partner's keeping an eye on them. I think one of the ladies went somewhere to make tea. Er, I was wondering, sir," he shuffled his feet nervously, "now that you're here . . . We was due off at six, you see, and—"

"You'll have to wait until your station sends someone to relieve you." Blade smiled bleakly. "Nice bit of overtime, eh, lad? In the meantime, you stay here. Nobody goes in or out of the building apart from members of the investigation."

Behind the constable, the door opened to admit a lanky figure muffled in a dark blue quilted anorak. "And about time too," Blade growled. "What kept you?"

The newcomer pulled back his hood to reveal a mop of ruffled fair hair crowning a fresh, freckled face that glowed with health, and a long, straight nose. The slate grey eyes were bright and clear even at this early hour. Although only an inch shorter than Blade, his slim athletic body, that of a long-distance runner, made him appear much smaller.

"Good morning, sir," John Hyde said, grinning cheerfully. "I came as quickly as I could. I don't live just around the corner like you."

The smile vanished when he saw his superintendent's scowl.

"Don't get smart with me, Sergeant," snapped Blade, and indicating for Hyde to follow, went back to the chest.

Waving a hand towards the pathologist, he said, "Dr Stoker, this is John Hyde, my new sergeant, who has kindly deigned to join us at last." He paused. "And I'll bet he's had a nice breakfast."

"Well," Hyde shifted uncomfortably, "Becky cooked it for me, so I couldn't just go out and leave it." Meeting the superintendent's bleak gaze, he added weakly, "Could I?"

Blade snorted. "Twenty-four years old, and thinks he knows it all. Newly promoted and newly wed. He's only been married three weeks."

"Ah!" The pathologist shook his head sadly. "I'm afraid it won't last, Sergeant. You'll see. After a year or so there won't be any breakfasts when you get called out in the middle of the night. She'll just turn over and go back to sleep — if she even bothers to wake up at all." He gave the young detective's arm a friendly squeeze. "Welcome to the madhouse."

Blade clapped his hands together. "Right. That's enough chat. There's work to be done. Perhaps it's just as well you *have* had breakfast, Sergeant, because I don't know when you'll get your next meal. First, you can get statements from the cleaning ladies who found the body. They're in a room through there." He nodded towards the corridor. "When you've taken their statements, tell them to go home. We don't want them cleaning up any evidence. Then you can fix us up with an incident room. There must be a suitable place here — a conference room perhaps — that can be made available to us."

Blade looked around. "And then get that film." He pointed to a CCTV camera that was mounted high up in the opposite corner of the hall, its lens directed straight at them — and at the chest. "It ought to tell us a lot."

"Yes, sir. I'll wake a few people up and get on with it," said Sergeant Hyde.

"And as soon as the scene-of-crime team are done and I can move the body, I'll see if this gentleman has any ID on him," Stoker said.

The three men peered down into the chest.

4

"You needn't bother, Fred," Blade said quietly. "His name is — was — Chief Superintendent Harold Ashington of Scotland Yard. And he was no gentleman. I'll see you later, Sergeant."

He turned on his heel, strode rapidly to the door, nodded to the constable, and was gone.

"Your boss seems out of sorts today," the pathologist commented. "I've never known him to be so grumpy. Ralph's usually a most genial chap." He stroked his chin thoughtfully. "Perhaps it's something to do with our customer in the chest. Obviously, he knows him." The thought seemed to worry the pathologist. "When he first saw the body, I thought he was going to pass out. Mind you, I don't envy him his job." He spread his arms. "Here we are in Bramshill, the world-famous police college, and he has a death on his plate. I need to examine the body, but my guess is that it will turn out to be murder. And not only is the victim a senior police officer, but probably some of the suspects will outrank him. A rather tricky situation for our detective superintendent, don't you think?" Stoker's eyes twinkled. "And for you, too, eh, John?"

"Could be, Doctor," The sergeant answered gloomily. "I'd better go and see those ladies, or I'll be in more trouble."

"Call me Fred," Stoker said genially. "No need for formality. Our paths will probably cross quite a lot from now on. Don't worry about the super though, his bark's worse than his bite. He used to pull your predecessor Percy Parrack's leg mercilessly — but it was Blade that got him his early promotion to DI. You're lucky to have him as your boss."

* * *

Outside, Blade pulled the heavy door shut behind him and leaned back against it. He closed his eyes and drew in a deep breath of cold frosty air, which sent him into a fit of coughing. Muttering a curse, he ran down to his car, which was parked at the foot of the broad stone steps leading from the mansion. He sat behind the steering wheel, then thumped it with his fist.

"What the hell are you playing at, Julie? What's going on? What have you bloody done?" He tried to think back to the previous night. Had his wife lied to him? He'd got home just after midnight, but Julie wasn't in. She arrived ten minutes later, saying she'd had a headache and had driven to the common to get some fresh air.

He had no reason to doubt her, but his mind slipped automatically into detective mode. A walk in the dark? Near midnight on a lonely, freezing cold common? There had been a heavy frost. Wouldn't the grass have been soaking wet? Yet he had noticed that her shoes were clean and dry.

Blade put the car in gear and made a U-turn, pausing briefly when the lights of two approaching vehicles blinded him. That would be the scene-of-crime team arriving. He was in no mood to speak to them. John Hyde and Fred Stoker could put them in the picture.

He turned into the long, narrow drive that cut through park and woodland to the main A30. After that, it was just five miles to his home on the outskirts of the village of Hartley Wintney.

CHAPTER TWO

RALPH BLADE covered the five miles at speed with a mounting sense of dread. The wide, main street with its eclectic selection of businesses, including plenty of antique shops, was deserted at this hour. He drove through the village, passing its two duck ponds and cricket field and turned into his drive. The dashboard clock read 07.23 and the night was giving way to a bleak grey dawn. Small white flakes heralding the first winter snow made hesitant exploratory darts towards the windscreen.

As he hung up his duffel coat in the hall, he could hear the clink of china being unloaded from the dishwasher. Julie was up. She turned to face him, surprised, as he entered the kitchen.

"What are you doing home so soon? I thought—"

"What's going on, Julie? And don't give me any more stories about headaches and walks on the common. Where did you really go last night?"

Her hand flew to her mouth. "I . . . I told you, I—"

He broke in again. "Have you seen or been in touch with Harold Ashington? Were you with him last night?"

"No!" she shouted. "I haven't seen him." Her face, already pale, was suddenly ashen.

"I really hope you're telling the truth," Blade said grimly, "because the bastard was murdered last night. I know because I've just seen his corpse. And I'm the bloody investigating officer."

"Oh my God." Staring at him, aghast, his wife drew a chair from under the kitchen table and sank on to it, covering her face with her hands. She looked up. "He rang me yesterday. He threatened me, said I had to see him at ten last night — he seemed to know you'd be out. I said he couldn't come here, so he said he'd meet me at the King's Head in Hartley. I waited there till nearly midnight, but he didn't turn up, so I came home. You were already in, so . . . so, yes, I lied and said I'd had a headache. I didn't dare tell you the truth. I thought . . . I thought you'd storm out and find him and do something silly. I thought you'd kill him."

Blade shook his head in disbelief. It was almost laughable. His wife feared that he might murder Ashington, while *he* suspected that she had actually done so. In a flash, awareness of the solid strength of their marriage engulfed him as he realised that each would go to any length to protect the other. And Julie had been right. If he had known about Ashington's telephone call, he probably would have done "something silly". She was trying to protect Blade from himself.

"You say he threatened you. How?"

"He . . . he mentioned Richard. Said we should talk. That we . . ." Her voice shook, and tears trickled from her eyes.

Her husband sat down facing her. Her clenched fists were resting on the table between them. They looked small and defenceless. He leaned forward and covered them with his own huge hand.

"Easy, love, easy." His voice was gentle now. "We'll get it sorted out, you'll see. But first you must try to remember exactly what was said. The phone rang, you picked it up — and?" Blade raised his eyebrows and gave her an encouraging smile.

She hesitated, unable to control the tremble in her voice. "He said, 'Guess who, Julie, a voice from the past.' He didn't have to say who it was. I'll never forget that voice. I said, 'Go away. You've no right to ring me.' He said, 'Don't hang up on me, Julie, or you'll regret it. And so will your husband. Just remember that I can wreck his career.'"

She raised her eyes to meet her husband's. "Can he?"

He shook his head. "Not now. It was all so long ago. They'd consider it trivial after all this time, unimportant. But go on."

She frowned. "He said: 'I miss you, Julie. It's time we got back together. You can be nice to me again, the way you used to be. *He* needn't know.' I said, 'In your dreams.' I was just about to hang up when he said, 'I'll ruin your precious Ralph Blade — and don't forget Richard.'"

She paused. Blade could feel her fists tighten beneath his own. She was struggling to control her tears. He leaned forward, closer to her.

"Richard?" — an incredulous shout. "He spoke about Richard?"

Julie nodded. "I felt sick." Her voice grew stronger. "I didn't think he even knew Richard existed. I said, 'What do you mean?' and he laughed and said, 'I met him in Loughborough. Nice lad. Handsome too. Who do you think he takes after, you or his dad? I must say he reminds me of myself when I was his age. But we'll talk about everything when we meet tonight. Ten o'clock at the King's Head. Be there. Or else.' And then he hung up."

She slid her hands from beneath Blade's and brought them up to her face. "My God, Ralph. He thinks he's Richard's father!"

"Thought," Blade corrected grimly. "The bugger's dead."

His mobile bleeped and he pulled it from his pocket. The text message read: "Meet ASAP, my office. Oliver."

* * *

9

Blade got back in the car, his mind in turmoil. All his earlier worries had now been crowded out by new, bigger ones. Richard. His son's name echoed in his head.

Blade was proud of his son, who was studying chemistry at Loughborough University and full of ideas for future projects. "You never know," he'd once joked to his parents, "I might invent a marbled kitchen work surface made of paper. When I'm a multi-millionaire I'll buy you a country mansion."

Richard . . . almost as tall as Blade but slender like his mother. with fine features and colouring just like Julie's.

And just like Harold Ashington's.

Trying to push the thought away, Blade drove on towards Basingstoke and Chief Superintendent Stan Oliver. What would he say to his chief? He tried to marshal his thoughts, but Harold Ashington kept getting in the way.

"The bastard!" he shouted.

Ashington *couldn't* be Richard's father.

Could he?

Figures had never been Blade's strong point. He tried to work out the timing of Julie's pregnancy, but his thoughts kept getting tangled.

"Bugger," he muttered, narrowly avoiding ramming the back of a Waitrose lorry. The combination of mathematics and driving was too dangerous. He jabbed at the CD player and Led Zeppelin flooded the car at full volume — not his choice, but this album was one of Richard's favourites. At least it was loud enough to drown out further thought.

He overtook the Waitrose lorry, and at just 9.15 a.m. was pulling up in the police station car park.

* * *

Chief Superintendent Stanley Oliver was, as always, immaculately turned out. Uniform neatly pressed, shirt with its starched collar so white it almost glowed. Like a halo that had slipped down around his neck, Blade had once joked.

Oliver was a dapper man, with one of those annoyingly trim waistlines that never changed no matter how many business lunches he consumed. At five feet nine, his weight was a constant eleven stone. There was no trace of grey in his spruce dark hair and his unlined boyish face made him look a decade younger than his forty-five years.

The two men were friends. In their twenties and early thirties, they had played together in the Hampshire police rugby team, Blade as a flanker in the forwards, and Oliver on the left wing. Oliver was still remembered for his speed and fierce tackles.

He waved towards a chair. "Take a seat, Ralph. Sorry to drag you in, but this looks like being quite a case, and the chief constable has been bending my ear since the crack of dawn. He's very keen for you to handle it, by the way. He thinks a lot of you, and it's on your patch."

Blade sighed. "That may be so, sir, but there may be a conflict of interest. I knew the victim."

"I'm aware of that. I've been on the phone to your sergeant, and he said you'd identified the man as Harold Ashington, a chief super in the Met. But the chief constable really wants us to deal with this ourselves without any interference from Scotland Yard. And I don't think the fact that you knew Ashington makes any difference."

"No, you don't understand. There was bad blood between us. It was because of him that I left the Met, way back when I was a rookie constable and he was a sergeant."

"So?"

Blade chewed his lip. "Okay. I suppose I'll have to tell you." He paused, trying to decide just how much to tell. "Look, the man was a bully and a blackmailer. Julie, who was also a constable in the Met in those days, had been going out with him but she dumped him in favour of me. He was furious, of course, and threatened to 'get' me. One night, a couple of weeks later, when Julie was off duty, he put me on a beat that took me past her house. Knowing I wouldn't be able to resist popping in to see her, the cunning piece of crap followed me and took a timed and dated photo of me going in through the front door. The next day he showed me the picture and threatened to report me. He said that if I didn't get out of London, he'd make sure my career was finished. I believed him. I was young then, still a bit wet behind the ears, and I didn't realise that such action would reflect badly on him too." Blade paused. "I knew there was a vacancy in Hampshire, and I was lucky enough to get it. I think the fact that I played rugby, and they were looking for likely team members, swung it for me. Ashington thought he'd have a clear field to win Julie back, but what he didn't know was that Julie had put in her own resignation so she could come with me. She didn't ask for a transfer because she was pregnant, and we got married soon after we moved. After Richard was born, she never considered re-joining the force. She loved just being a mum."

Blade stopped speaking, wondering whether to tell of Ashington's phone call to Julie. He decided against it. "That's it really. I have heard rumours over the years that Ashington got promotions either by sycophancy or by uncovering his superior's salacious secrets and threatening to reveal them. The man was a total toerag."

"Hmm." Oliver scratched his head thoughtfully. "I'll report the gist of what you've told me to the chief, but I still don't see why it should prevent you from heading the investigation." He grinned. "Anyway, I know you didn't kill the man. I'm your alibi. Yesterday we had lunch together here before a meeting about budget cuts that dragged on until after six. Then I drove behind you to Winchester to attend Billy Buxton's farewell. Your sergeant — he seems to be a bright lad, what's his name?"

"John Hyde. Newly promoted and just joined my team."

"Ah, yes, Hyde. Well, when I rang Bramshill just before you got here he told me that the pathologist has estimated Ashington's time of death as being somewhere around mid-afternoon yesterday. So, there you are, Ralph — eliminated from police enquiries."

Oliver stood up and held out his hand to Blade. "Good luck, Ralph. The chief constable said to tell you to ask for any extra help you might need. I'll let you know his reaction to what you've just told me, but I'm sure it will be the same as mine. Keep me in touch with progress. I've alerted your team, including a new member we've given you, Detective Inspector Dorothy Fraser from HQ. Do you know her?" Blade shook his head. "You'll like her. She's a good 'un, came to us a few months ago from somewhere up north. Anyway, the team will already be waiting for you at Bramshill. But don't forget, if you want any more help, just ask. This case is on our patch, and the chief wants *us* to clear it up quickly, before the Met have a chance to poke their noses in."

The fourteen miles that separated divisional HQ from Bramshill took just twenty-three minutes via the A33. Halfway there, Blade pulled into a lay-by to read a text on his phone. It was from Oliver: "Chief says carry on. Every confidence in you."

CHAPTER THREE

JOHN HYDE had been busy. Back at Bramshill, Blade found him in one of the four lecture rooms situated behind the reception. His sergeant greeted him with a grin.

"Bit of luck here, boss, a ready-made, on-the-spot incident room. It's a mock-up for students' lectures and exercises and the commandant says we can use it for the real thing."

Blade was impressed. All the members of the team, plus several civilian workers, were seated at desks already equipped with phones and computers. A white display board had been started with crime scene pictures including a photo of Harold Ashington.

He smiled. "Well done, John. Sorry I left you in the lurch earlier. Things I had to sort out."

His sergeant grinned happily, grateful for the praise. "We can use the room next door too. It's got a long table and chairs — ideal for our conferences on progress and tactics. And there's an offshoot from it that you could make your own office."

"Excellent. I'll do that." Blade clapped his hands loudly — a habit that John Hyde was beginning to find mildly irritating — and everyone in the room turned to face him.

"Hullo. Nice to see you all again. Let's go next door and get this show on the road."

He turned to lead the way, and with a noisy scraping of chairs, the team found places at the long table. Hyde tugged at his chief's sleeve.

"A quick word first, sir?"

They moved away from the table. "What is it?"

"Perhaps we should wait a bit before we start. I didn't have time to tell you before, but they've sent an inspector from HQ to join us. She must have gone to powder her nose or something, but I expect she'll be back in a minute."

"Oh yes, that will be Detective Inspector Dorothy Fraser. I've been told about her. What's she like?"

"Well, if I wasn't a married man, I wouldn't mind—"

"I heard that, Sergeant."

They swung around to see a woman standing in the doorway. The chunky yellow sweater and beige corduroy trousers tucked into sheepskin-lined boots failed to conceal her athletic figure. Her shoulder-length dark chestnut hair was pulled back into a ponytail, exposing a complexion that had no need of make-up. Blade guessed her to be about twenty-seven.

"Ears like a bat," he whispered softly to Hyde.

"I heard that, too. *Sir.*"

Her angry gaze focused on her superintendent, who had been trying to place her accent. Now he had it. His puzzled expression cleared as he recognised the Tyneside twang. She was a Geordie. He opened his mouth to speak, but she was still talking.

"Did you know, bats have a biological sonar system called echolocation? They can make ultrasonic sounds that bounce off objects, even in the dark, allowing them to work out in split seconds the exact location, size and nature of the objects." She paused, and the two men exchanged uncertain glances. "But I'm not that good, sir. I didn't *really* hear you whisper that." Her tight lips suddenly parted in a wide smile, revealing even, white teeth. Her clear, hazel eyes sparkled with merriment. "I read your lips. You see, when I was a little girl me mam went deaf and I went with her to her lip-readin' lessons, so I picked it oop."

She stepped towards her new chief, hand extended. "Hello, sir, me name is—"

"I know who you are, Inspector. Dorothy. May I call you Dorothy?" She nodded and he shook her hand, smiling sheepishly. "Your lip-reading talent could come in handy in our line of business."

"Aye, it does, especially when suspects start whispering together. Once I had a feller under surveillance in a pub in South Shields — that's where I come from — and he went to sit at a table with two other guys. I couldn't believe it. They were discussin' the details of a raid they were planning on a sub-post office: date, time, everything. I got it all. So, when they did the job, we were ready and waiting. We nicked the lot of 'em." She laughed. "And, the funny thing was, I'd had him under observation for something completely different."

"That's a great story, Dorothy, but now we've got work to do." He gestured towards the table. "Grab a seat."

* * *

Blade allowed his gaze to roam over the team. He liked and trusted them all and was familiar with their various strengths and weaknesses. The two detective constables, Bill Headley and Anthony Robinson, worked well together but were complete opposites.

Headley, a balding, fatherly figure in his late fifties, was nearing retirement. He had never married and was content to live alone in the neat country cottage left to him by his parents, who had both died in a traffic accident when he was just twenty-one.

He spent all his holidays hillwalking in North Wales, the Lakes or Scotland, something that never made any impression on an expanding waistline due to the real ale he consumed when listening to his extensive collection of CDs. His taste in music was eclectic, from pop to classical, depending entirely on his mood of the moment.

Temperamentally, Headley was ideally suited to his work, being methodical and meticulous. But he had one big flaw. His obvious passion for the job was matched only by his determination to avoid all responsibility, and over the years he had firmly rejected every offer of promotion. He was a happy man.

Anthony Robinson, on the other hand, was ambitious. Having graduated from university with a first class honours degree in law and politics, he had decided on a career in the police force. After two years he passed the sergeants' exam with ease and his quick mind and natural ability earned him a transfer to CID. There, he was partnered with Bill Headley, a move that genuinely pleased him, because he knew he could learn a lot from the older man. Now he hoped that before long he would make it to sergeant, the first rung on the promotion ladder that he aimed to climb to the top.

Blade watched him settle beside Bill. They made an odd pair: short, tubby, round-faced Headley with his habitual genial expression alongside the tall, slim and darkly handsome Robinson. The superintendent knew Anthony had been disappointed when John Hyde had been brought in to fill the vacancy for sergeant. He wondered if his ambitious young colleague had accepted his assurance that he was in the running for one of two detective sergeant posts due to become vacant within the next year or so. He ought to. At almost twenty-four he would probably be the youngest sergeant on the force.

The other pair seated at the table were also young. Looking pleased to be in plain clothes, they were constables on loan from Uniform, and were both hoping for permanent transfer to CID.

Adrian Harper, just under six feet tall, was all muscle. He had the massive shoulders of a rugby prop forward. His close-cropped dark hair emphasised ears that had been pummelled so often in scrums that they resembled a pair of storm-battered television dishes. His nose had likewise been rearranged so many times that it was impossible to guess at its original shape, and it didn't appear to belong to Harper's craggy face. It sat, like a lump of putty, above a broad mouth and strong, jutting chin. However, these features were redeemed by his friendly brown eyes and good-humoured smile, which softened his features and made people forget his ugliness.

Beauty and the beast, Blade thought unkindly, smiling inwardly as he saw Lucy Ramsay, the second constable on loan from Uniform, edge her chair closer to that of Harper, whose battered appearance served to emphasise her elegance. Shoulder-length natural blonde hair framed the pale perfection of her face, large grey-green eyes and long, straight nose above generous lips that curved up in a pleasant smile. She was wearing jeans and a green polo-neck jumper.

Lucy had left school with excellent grades in chemistry, physics and maths, but had no desire to spend three or four years studying at university. She had decided, while a fifth former, that she wanted to serve the community. And she believed she had the ability to achieve senior rank in the police service.

Blade clapped his hands again, this time to silence the scraping of chairs and the low murmur of chatter. "Right, folks, let's get started. We're investigating what appears to be the murder of Chief Superintendent Harold Ashington of the Met. Sergeant Hyde has been here since early this morning and I'm sure he's already put you in the picture." He nodded towards his colleague. "So, John, bring us all up to date."

Hyde stood up. "Not many positives to report so far. The victim was in Syndicate Six, the senior command course at Bramshill led by a former chief constable, Felicity Dumble. It seems that Mr Ashington was about to be promoted to commander at the Met. And it is definitely murder — he was poisoned with cyanide. The pathologist rang about half an hour ago to confirm it, and he estimates the time of death to be between two and four o'clock yesterday afternoon."

Blade looked puzzled. "As early as that? It seems odd that the body wasn't discovered until the cleaners arrived this morning. What about the CCTV? Any joy there?"

"I was busy getting us fixed up here, so I got DC Headley to look into that. Did you find anything, Bill?"

Headley rose to his feet. "Nothing yet. I retrieved the film from the camera that's focused on the chest where the victim was found and ran it through at speed, starting from eight p.m. But there's something odd. Until about ten o'clock there was plenty of activity with students going in and out — probably visiting the library — all passing close to the chest. The lid was up, as usual, and if there had been a body inside, surely someone would have noticed. After all, they're all coppers — and being on courses here, supposedly bright ones earmarked for promotion. Anyway, they'll have been trained to observe. So, I'm convinced the chest was empty at that time. Yet, from just after ten until the cleaners arrived at four thirty-five a.m., there was no movement. The picture was still. Apparently, nobody — and specifically no *body* — went near that chest. I've just started to go through the footage again, at slow speed this time, to see if I've missed anything. Obviously, that's going to take hours."

Headley was about to sit down when he straightened up again. "The security manager, a chap called Roger Cotter, personally looks after the CCTV. I'm told he's an expert, so I'll have a word with him tomorrow. He's been away for a few days, fishing somewhere in the wilds, and he can't be contacted — his mobile has been switched off. He's due back here in the morning and usually arrives about seven thirty."

"Thank you, Bill," said Blade. "I shall want to speak to Mr Cotter too. Ask his staff to tell him I want to see him as soon as he gets in. Meanwhile, keep working on the CCTV film. Lucy and Adrian, I want you to check all the students in Syndicate Six — delve into their careers and backgrounds. Try to find if there was ever a link between any of them and

Harold Ashington in the past, or if there's been any trouble between them during their time here."

Lucy couldn't hide her delight at being partnered with Adrian. But Harper didn't look so happy.

Blade grinned. "Don't worry, Adrian. I know they're all senior officers, but don't let them bully you. Just let them know that you're the one investigating the murder and 'eliminating them from police inquiries.' Anyway, one look at you and *they'll* be the ones that are terrified."

Adrian, who was used to having his leg pulled about his battered appearance, tried unsuccessfully to crack his battered face into a smile. He made no comment.

Blade glanced at his watch. "And now, you lucky people, Sergeant Hyde has arranged a free lunch for you. I'm sure you can find your way to the dining hall."

As they left the conference room and made their way outside, the sergeant and Dorothy Fraser fell into step beside him.

"The commandant seems quite anxious to see you, sir," Hyde said. "He asked if you could go to his office at two thirty."

"Oh, right. What's he like?"

"Not too happy about a having a murder in his college. I have a feeling he thinks the Yard should be handling it. But he's decent enough and has been very helpful."

"I see. Hmm . . . two thirty it is, then. Dorothy, you'd better come with me for moral support. Between us we can convince him we're better than the Yard and—"

A loud rendition of *Für Elise* emanated from his pocket. He pulled out his mobile. The call was from his wife.

"I'll have to take this," he said, turning to face away while the others walked on a few yards and then stood, waiting.

He spoke quietly into the phone. "What is it, Julie? You know I'm—"

"It's Richard!" she cut in, and he could almost feel the desperation in her voice.

"What do you mean, it's Richard?"

"He's here. And he knows."

"Knows what?"

"About Harold Ashington. About the murder. About the King's Head. He was there last night. And he saw me there—"

"I'll be with you in ten minutes." Blade ended the call and re-joined his companions.

"Something has come up," he said. "You two enjoy your lunch and, Dorothy, I'll see you just before two thirty in the incident room."

CHAPTER FOUR

HE SPENT the short drive to his home in a whirl of thoughts and questions. Why was Richard at the King's Head? What time did he arrive there? Why didn't he speak to his mother when he saw her there? And the niggling doubt that had wormed into his mind since early morning to trigger the biggest question of all:

Who is Richard?

Was he the son he had always loved and admired? Or . . . ? The alternative answer was unthinkable.

Blade parked the car in the drive, hurried into the house and headed straight for the sitting room, where Richard — with a cry of "Dad!" — propelled himself from his armchair to hug him. "No matter what, you'll always be my dad. Always have been and always will be."

Blade stood stiffly, arms hanging by his sides. He half raised them, then let them drop again. He looked across the room at his wife.

"What have you told him?"

"Everything. I had to."

He took a step back, releasing himself from Richard's embrace.

"Sit down," he said coldly.

Richard retreated slowly, his face a confused mask of hurt and disbelief, and slumped back into his chair.

Blade towered over him. "What the hell has been going on between you and Ashington?"

"Nothing. I . . . I thought he was a friend of yours."

"So how did you get to know him?"

"He bumped into me in a bar, in Loughborough. Spilt my beer, so he bought me a fresh one. We got talking and he mentioned that he was a senior police officer at Scotland Yard. I said my dad was a policeman, too. He asked my name, and it turned out he knew you."

"What was he doing in Loughborough?" Blade asked.

"I don't know, I didn't ask. I supposed it was police business, or he might have a son or daughter at uni there."

"How come you never mentioned the man, when you thought he was a friend of mine?"

"I know it seems odd, but he asked me not to tell you. He kind of hinted that he might be able to do a big favour for you career-wise, but to keep mum about it so it would be a big surprise and . . ." Richard sat up suddenly. "Why are you questioning me like this? Like I'm one of your murder suspects?"

"Because," Blade said wearily, "you *are*, or soon will be."

Richard sank back in the chair again, looking miserable. "You can't really believe I killed him."

"What were you doing at the King's Head last night?" Blade's face remained stony, his voice was harsh.

"Mr Ashington rang me early yesterday morning, before eight o'clock, and told me he was at Bramshill. He said he'd booked a room for me at the King's Head. I should be there no later than nine o'clock that night and must stay in the room until he came to fetch me. He said we'd give you and Mum a big surprise. That was the first time he ever mentioned her."

"What time did you get there?" Blade asked.

"About half past eight."

"What time did you leave Loughborough?"

"I caught the ten fifteen train, which got into Euston at twelve twenty."

"What did you do between then and eight thirty?"

Richard shrugged. "I just wandered around London, seeing the sights."

"Did you see anyone, speak to anyone who might remember you around midday or two o'clock? Think, boy. Times could be important."

Richard shook his head. "I queued to buy a sandwich from a shop at about one, but I didn't speak to anybody. It was busy, so I doubt if the girl on the checkout would remember me."

"Okay. Now, tell me about last night. Everything, from the time you got to the King's Head."

"I booked in with the landlord and he gave me the key, directed me to the room and said Mr Ashington had paid my bed and breakfast fee in advance. I don't know what he was thinking, but the way he kept looking at me made me feel very uncomfortable. Anyway, I went up, dumped my backpack on the bed and went straight back to the bar because I was hungry. I ordered a meat pie and chips with a pint, ate quickly and was back in my room just a few minutes after nine. I waited and waited, but Mr Ashington never showed. When it turned eleven o'clock, I was really fed up, so I decided to go down to see if the bar was still open. It was. But I didn't go in because when I opened the door the first person I saw was Mum." He glanced uncertainly at his mother. "She was by herself and I thought she must be waiting for you, but there was still no sign of Mr Ashington. I remembered what he had told me and went back upstairs. By one o'clock, when he still hadn't come for me, I was really worried, and I went down again, but the bar was in darkness and there was nobody about. I went up to bed then, but I didn't get any sleep. This morning, when the landlord served me my breakfast, I asked him if he'd seen Mr Ashington last night. He said he hadn't. I didn't know what to do. I couldn't ring him because he never gave me his mobile number. I knew I had to vacate my room by eleven, so I went up to pack my stuff. I thought about trying to find Bramshill's number and asking for him, and then . . ." The young man's voice broke. "And then . . . the radio in my room was tuned into the local station and a newscaster interrupted the music to say the body of a man had been found in the main building of the Police Staff College at Bramshill. The unnamed dead man was thought to be a senior Scotland Yard officer, and Hampshire murder squad detectives were investigating. I panicked when I heard that. I grabbed my backpack and went down to check out. The radio was on downstairs, so the landlord must have heard the newsflash too. He kept giving me very strange looks and I could tell he was about to say something, so . . . so I got out of there. And I came home," he finished lamely.

Blade swore silently, wondering how the media had picked it up so quickly. Probably those bloody cleaning women, he thought. Hyde would have warned them to keep quiet, but the temptation to shoot their mouths off would have been irresistible. What now? Richard's account had been plausible. He was always straightforward, open, honest. He'd never been devious.

"All right, son," he said. There was less chill in his voice now. "I'll do what I can to keep your name out of this mess, though right now I can't see how. You'd better get back to Loughborough. Keep your head down and don't talk about this to anyone."

He went over to his wife and took her hands in his. "Julie, drive him to Fleet and get him on the first train to London. Don't worry, we'll get through this somehow, but I can't stop now. I've got to get back to Bramshill for a meeting at two thirty."

CHAPTER FIVE

BLADE ENTERED the incident room and almost cannoned into the newest member of his team.

"Sir!" Dorothy couldn't hide her excitement. "There's been a development. We have a name, a possible suspect. I was just on my way to interview an informant. I'm taking Sergeant Hyde, who's gone to fetch the car, but now that you're here? I know you're tied up right now because you're due to see the commandant in a few minutes, and I thought—"

"Names," Blade interrupted. "Who is this informant, and what's the name of the possible suspect?"

She pulled a notebook from her pocket. "I took the call from a Gerald Harptree, who is the landlord of the King's Head. He said a young man stayed at the pub last night. He was booked in and paid for in advance by an older person whose name the landlord doesn't know, but he does know that he's a senior police officer on a course at Bramshill. The two were supposed to meet last night, and he thought there must be a bit of hanky-panky going on. But the older one didn't turn up. When Mr Harptree heard the news on the radio this morning, he put two and two together and decided to ring us. He said the young man, who seemed very jumpy, was booked in as Mr R. Blade. Oh." Dorothy's hand flew to her mouth. She joked: "Ee! Your namesake. You haven't got a murderer in the family, have you, sir?"

Blade was in no mood for levity. His mind was reeling under this latest blow. If his son were to become a suspect — possibly the prime suspect — his own position would become untenable. But if he handed over the investigation to someone else, he would no longer be in a position to protect his family. He needed time to think.

As the seconds ticked by, he became aware that John Hyde had entered the room and was standing beside Dorothy, who was still awaiting his reply. He decided to play for time.

"I think your Mr Harptree can wait another hour or so. I'd like you to come with me to see the commandant. You too, John," Blade added with a nod to the sergeant. "Have your pen ready. You can take notes."

* * *

The three of them climbed the stone steps to the heavy oak door of the mansion. John Hyde opened it and his senior colleagues preceded him into the hall, deserted now except for a solitary uniformed constable. The wooden chest, still open but void of its unwelcome guest, had been isolated by blue-and-white tape. Entry to the main interior of the building, through arches to left and right of the hall, was also blocked.

Blade acknowledged the constable's salute and was directed to an office immediately to the left of the front entrance. He led the way, pausing in the doorway to allow his eyes to adjust to the gloom. There was nobody in the room, which was small. A desk and several filing cabinets made the space even more cramped. A splash of bright light that spilled from a much larger inner office further illuminated the room, itself lit only by feeble wintry daylight filtering through the single window.

From where he stood in the doorway, Blade got the weird impression that he was looking at a pair of china figurines. The man on the left had shiny black hair and a moustache above a pair of thin lips and a lantern jaw. The woman, equally shiny, had long blonde hair pinned up, which emphasised her elegant high cheekbones and red lips.

The man stood up. "Ah, Superintendent." His voice shook the detective out of his whimsy. These two were no delicate ornaments but ordinary flesh and blood. The man glanced at his watch. "Come through, you're right on time. I thought you'd be alone. Er, Sergeant Hyde I know, but—"

"This is Detective Inspector Dorothy Fraser," Blade said. "I brought them with me so that they would be fully apprised of what you can tell us without me having to repeat it all later."

"Good, good. I'm Roderick Chaytor-Gill, Bramshill's commandant, as you've probably guessed, and this," he indicated the woman who had risen to stand beside him, "is Felicity Dumble, my colleague and deputy, currently the director of Syndicate Six, which, as I'm sure you're aware, is the senior command course our murder victim was attending." He added proudly, "Mrs Dumble was herself once a student here and has served as a chief constable."

The commandant gestured towards a chair that had been placed in front of his desk. "Take a seat, Superintendent. Sergeant Hyde, can you bring a couple of chairs from my secretary's office for yourself and Inspector Fraser?" Nodding towards a large settee that stood against the wall behind the desk, he joked: "We could drag the sofa over, but it might be too comfortable and send you to sleep."

While Hyde was busy fetching the chairs, the two college heads chatted to Dorothy, and Blade studied Chaytor-Gill. Although he had never met the man before, he was familiar with his background because, when the commandant had first been appointed, the local press had reported his career in full — and, as a policeman, Blade had read it with great interest.

With public school- and Oxford-educated Chaytor-Gill's first class honours master's degree followed by a doctorate, he was all set for a comfortable life in academia. And then, suddenly, inexplicably, he turned his back on it all and joined the Metropolitan Police. There, his talents were soon noted, and he was fast-tracked through the ranks, soon rising to chief superintendent. When the post of commandant at Bramshill became vacant, he applied and was successful. "The police service and academia rolled into one," a delighted Chaytor-Gill was reported to have said.

Smartly dressed in a bespoke dark blue suit, he was tall and slim, with the friendly, easy grace and confidence common to men used to being obeyed. Blade took an instant and instinctive dislike to him. He wondered unkindly if the man's shiny black hair was dyed.

As John Hyde brought Dorothy her chair and went to fetch another for himself, Blade switched his attention to Felicity Dumble. He had doubts, too, about her blonde hair. It was dark at the roots. She wore it pinned up, business-like, exposing a face that was beginning to need the help of a little make-up to disguise the onset of lines. She was wearing a mid-green blouse and beige skirt and looked a decade younger than her forty-four years. Blade found her attractive, and he smiled inwardly at himself, recognising that perhaps there was an element of jealousy in his reaction to her companion.

When the commandant mentioned that Felicity had been a chief constable, it jogged Blade's memory. After the police forces of two counties had been merged in a money saving exercise, she had declined the offer to serve as deputy to her male opposite number who got the top job. The story had made the national press, which later also reported her move to Bramshill with details of her age and high-flying career in the police service after leaving Cambridge University with a first class honours degree in law and politics. Blade had read both of those reports, too.

With everyone finally settled around the desk, the commandant apologised for not offering his visitors coffee, because his secretary wasn't there to make it.

"I sent her home yesterday morning. The poor girl's suffering . . . flu, I wouldn't be surprised."

His deputy gave a short, scornful laugh. "Ha! The only thing wrong with the precious Miss Helena Willerby is a slight sniffle complicated, I suspect, by a large dose of work-shyness."

"Now, you know that's not true." Chaytor-Gill shot her a warning glance. "She's a hard worker, trustworthy. Been with me for years. I don't know why you're so against her. I sent her home yesterday because she was obviously ill—"

"What time would that be, sir?" Blade said, cutting him short.

The commandant blinked. "Tennish. Ten thirty perhaps. Well before the time of the murder, if that's what you're thinking."

"Um, yes, but we'll still need to talk to her. If you could give us her address?" Blade said, mildly.

"I'll get someone to look it up, but give the poor girl some time to get better," was the grumpy response. "I can't see how she can possibly help your inquiry in any case. On the other hand, the reason I've asked Mrs Dumble to join us is because she has some information that might *really* be relevant to your investigation."

The commandant assumed the friendly smile again. "Of course, we want to help in any way we can. We have expert detectives here, who lecture on the subject, all at your disposal. Mrs D and I have also spent much of our careers in CID."

Blade leaned forward, stroking his chin. "Er, yes. Sergeant Hyde has told me how helpful you've been, sir. The incident room and the other facilities are amazing and very much appreciated. But I'm sure you will understand that we can't accept any hands-on help in our inquiries."

The commandant dropped the smile. "Why on earth not?"

Blade's face was expressionless, his tone even. "Well, sir, as I'm sure you will agree, Bramshill is a murder scene. It's a fairly large but enclosed community and, until I can prove otherwise, everyone in it is a possible suspect."

The commandant's jaw dropped. He turned to his deputy. "Did you hear that? The man says we're murder suspects!"

"I'm sure he didn't mean it like that," she said. "He was just explaining the invidious position he's in. Weren't you?" She turned to Blade, raising an eyebrow.

"Precisely, ma'am," he said.

Chaytor-Gill grunted unhappily. "Well, if we can't help, what about the Met? Can't they be brought in?"

"My chief constable is keen for us to handle it ourselves. It's on our patch and I know we can cope," Blade said.

"That's as may be, but I warn you that I shall be pressing for the Yard to take over." The commandant's tone became conciliatory. "Look, I expect you know that Bramshill will be closing soon." Blade nodded. "Well, when we do close, I want it to be with a clean sheet, not with an unsolved murder hanging over us. For Pete's sake, we're respected as the finest police staff college in the world. We'll be a laughing stock if we can't solve our own murder."

"I don't think it'll come to that, sir." Blade changed the subject. "You said that Mrs Dumble has some information for us?"

"It could be nothing, it's up to you to decide," Felicity broke in quickly before her boss could reply. "Two days ago, a student on a junior command course came to me and made a complaint about Harold Ashington. She knows I head Syndicate Six, or perhaps she chose me simply because I'm a woman. Anyway, she alleged that he had been stalking her, and the previous evening had forced his way into her room and sexually assaulted her."

"Her name?" said Blade, glancing across to make sure his sergeant was taking notes.

"Inspector Angela Liddell. She's a very fit young lady — into karate according to her CV — and she managed to fight him off. I spoke to Ashington yesterday morning. He denied everything of course and claimed it was the other way around. He said she'd invited him into her room for a drink and had suggested that he might get her into the Met and help her up the career ladder. When he told her that was impossible, and that he was a happily married man, she turned nasty and stabbed him with a pair of nail scissors before he managed to escape."

John Hyde stopped writing. "That might tie in with the pathologist's report, sir. Things have been happening so fast I haven't had time to update you fully. As you know, the cause of death was confirmed as cyanide poisoning, but there was also an unexplained wound on the victim's left side as well as recent bruising to the groin. The wound was covered by a piece of fabric dressing, the sort you cut from a strip."

"Thank you, Sergeant." Blade looked at Mrs Dumble. "Thank you for your help. I'll speak to Inspector Liddell. I wonder, would there be a photograph of her somewhere, in her records perhaps?"

"I thought of that." With a smug smile, she leaned forward to open a folder on the desk. "I got this from the security office. It was taken for her identity tag. I've had it enlarged for you." Felicity handed over a photo of a young woman wearing a police inspector's uniform.

"That's great," Blade said and passed it to Hyde. "You can stick it on the board, John."

"It sounds like a good lead for you," said the commandant. "I don't suppose you've got very far yet."

"We're following several lines of enquiry, but my gut feeling is that we'll learn a lot from the CCTV. There's something odd going on there. I'll be seeing your head of security first thing in the morning."

"Roger Cotter?" Chaytor-Gill, brow furrowed, gave his deputy a quick glance. "Fine chap. Ex-army. What are you thinking? Surely you don't believe that he. . . . ?"

"I'm told he's the expert. Apparently he oversaw the installation of the CCTV a few years back. If anyone's been fiddling with the system, I reckon he's the man to spot it."

Blade looked around the room. "Nice place you have here, sir. But I'm surprised you've been allowed in, it being a crime scene and all that. I see access to the rest of the mansion has been taped off."

"Yes. Damned inconvenient, but it had to be done. All the other offices upstairs have been closed, and the staff were sent away before they had a chance to enter the building. Luckily, most of them can work from home. As for my own office, I had it relocated down here when I was appointed as commandant. It's conveniently near the front door. It's also away from the possible crime scene. I had a word with the forensics people, and they cleared this room and my secretary's office first, so that I could have access. I locked up when I left just after five thirty last evening and it was still locked this morning."

"So, it's unlikely that the murderer was in here," Felicity added. She laughed. "Unless it was a ghost. They can walk through walls and locked doors, can't they? But of course!" Her eyes widened in mock wonder. "It was the White Lady who dunnit! She's been seen before in the hall, near the mistletoe-bough chest, which would explain your CCTV mystery. A ghost wouldn't show up, would they?"

"Maybe not," said Blade drily, "but a thirteen-stone body would — and I don't think a spirit would be capable of lifting it into the chest."

"Who is this White Lady?" Dorothy asked.

"She's part of the history of Bramshill," the commandant said. "You tell them, Felicity."

"Well, briefly," she began, "this lovely home was built for Edward, Lord Zouche of Harringsworth in the early seventeenth century on the site of a fourteenth century manor house. In 1699 the mansion and its 269 acres of parkland was sold to Sir John Cope, a baronet whose descendants lived here until 1935, when it was bought by Lord Brocket. In 1953 the Home Office acquired the property, and an old oak chest, known as the mistletoe-bough chest, came with it as part of the deal. I believe it was brought over from Italy by one of the Cope family, the fifth baronet, I think, and it's been here ever since."

"Ee!" Dorothy interrupted, "That chest out there? Where the body was found? In the hall?"

Felicity nodded. "The very same. But it wasn't just the mistletoe-bough that came to stay. The ghost of a young Italian bride came too. Her name was Genevre Orsini, and her wedding took place on Christmas Eve, 1727. After the ceremony, she played a game of hide-and-seek with her new husband and their guests. She went off to find a hiding place and was never seen again until, fifty years later, her skeleton was found in an old wooden chest. She was still in her bridal gown, one hand clutching a sprig of mistletoe. When she'd lowered the lid on her hiding place the spring lock had snapped shut, trapping her. She was entombed for half a century." Felicity's voice became hushed. "From the moment that tomb was opened and her sad fate became known, it has been called the mistletoe-bough chest. Now the poor girl wanders around the mansion, looking sad — well, let's face it, she hasn't got much to be happy about, has she? She has often been seen in the Long Gallery, the Fleur de Lys room and the area around the chest out there." Felicity nodded towards the door. "She usually announces her presence with a pleasant aroma of lily of the valley."

The silence that followed was broken by a laugh. "Yeah, well, nice story," said John Hyde. "Pity there's no such thing as ghosts."

"You may say that, Sergeant," said Chaytor-Gill, "but there have been many sightings by credible witnesses, including members of the Cope family, a senior police officer from India on a course here in 1986, and King Michael of Romania, who lived in the house with his family in the early 1950s before the Home Office bought it. He had an exorcism carried out after Anne, his queen, saw the White Lady sitting in the king's room. It didn't work, though, because she's been seen since then."

Felicity Dumble leaned towards her chief and murmured something in his ear. The commandant looked at his watch and, smiling at his visitors, brought the meeting to a close. "That's all I have time for. Thank you for coming. I have to prepare for a meeting at the Home Office in the morning. There's a car coming for me at seven. Things to clear up before the closure."

"I'm sorry Bramshill's finishing, sir," Dorothy said, rising from her chair. "I'd hoped to come here one day." She gave a short laugh. "On a senior command course, naturally. Are there any plans for a new college?"

His reply was curt. "Nothing's settled, Inspector."

* * *

The rising wind added a sharp edge to the cold. Though it was only just turned three forty-five, it was already getting dark. Menacing thick black clouds threatened more snow. The three detectives hurried down the steps outside the mansion. Dorothy, almost trotting to keep up with Blade, wished she had put her parka on.

"I think there's a rabbit away there, sir," she said.

Blade stopped abruptly. "Rabbit? What do you mean?"

Dorothy wished she'd waited until they were comfortably back in the warm before making her remark. "Back there, when Mrs Dumble whispered to the commandant, she said, 'Time to prepare for tomorrow, Sir Rod.' And *he* said, 'Right. And time for me to make a lady of you.'"

Blade resumed walking, but more slowly. "So?"

"So, I reckon there's a rabbit away. Surely, with closure so near and the sale of Bramshill already decided, there can't be anything else to discuss. Can there? Well, nothing important enough to motor him all the way to London, unless there was something else to talk about. Like jobs, perhaps. Jobs that put the holders in line for a title? Just think what nice, ripe plums are handed out on the recommendation of the Home Office. One of those could make him a *sir*."

"Okay, so you think Chaytor-Gill and Mrs Dumble are having it off and he is after a plum job with a title. Anyway, he's married, it's his *wife* who'd be the lady, not his bit on the side. So what? It's got bugger all to do with us," Blade said. They entered their building and came to a halt in the corridor. "And you can stop grinning," he added, glaring at Hyde, who had been enjoying the exchange. "We are not here to indulge in, or in this case instigate, idle gossip. We're here to solve a murder."

"No, sir, um, yes, sir. I'll get this up on the board," said Hyde, hurrying, red-faced, towards the incident room, clutching the photograph of Inspector Angela Liddell.

"And I'll go and interview the pub landlord, sir," Dorothy said stiffly, still seething over her upbraiding in front of the sergeant. "He might have some more pertinent gossip. Sir."

She turned to go but Blade grasped her arm, pulling her around to face him. Throughout the interview with the commandant he had been wrestling with the problem of how to deal with the latest twist in his personal nightmare. Now his mind was made up.

"No. Come into my new office. There's something I must tell you."

She followed him, still resentful, through the conference room, past the long table and chairs to his prospective office. They seated themselves and sat in uncomfortable silence while Blade gathered his thoughts. He took a deep breath.

"As far as Mr Harptree is concerned, you can get his statement tomorrow, or even later, because I can tell you exactly what he's going to say." She looked astonished. He tried to smile but didn't do a very good job of it. "I know I've been pretty bloody, and I apologise, but when you've heard what I'm about to tell you, I hope you'll understand why, and that you'll forgive me. But first I must have your assurance that you won't repeat any of this to anyone without my prior consent. Do you agree to that?"

She nodded. Blade proceeded to tell her everything, including the details of his conversation with Chief

Superintendent Oliver earlier in the day. He even told her what he had omitted to tell Oliver — Ashington's telephone call to Julie, his contact with Richard in Loughborough and his belief that he was Richard's father.

"To be fair," Blade said wearily, "even I didn't know about Richard's involvement with Ashington until lunchtime — and I did offer to withdraw from the case because of a conflict of interest. I don't want to, of course. I want to be in a position to shield my family, establish their innocence while finding the killer. Anyway, both Mr Oliver and, apparently, the chief constable want me to carry on and," he paused, "I'd like to have you on my side, Dorothy. Together, we can crack this. Look, I'd rather you didn't mention the bits I haven't told him, but you're welcome to check with the chief super."

"Oh, believe me, I *will* check with him," she said. Then, her gloomy expression brightened, and she smiled. "But if he confirms what you say, and gives me the okay, I'll be happy to work with you, sir."

They looked up at the sound of a loud knock at the door. Sergeant Hyde, looking awkward, stood just inside the entrance. He apologised for interrupting and pointed out that it was now after five o'clock. Blade hadn't noticed.

"Of course," he said. "Tell everyone to go home, but they must be back here for seven thirty in the morning. We're going to be busy. And make sure you get a good night's sleep, John. It's been a long day."

"Right, sir," Hyde said, but remained in the doorway, shifting nervously from foot to foot. "Well, um, see you later then."

His boss stared blankly at him.

"About seven? The other day you said your wife wants to meet Becky and . . ."

The penny dropped. "Seven, yes, of course. Dinner. It slipped my mind for a moment. You'd better get off now."

As the sergeant made his escape, Blade wondered desperately if Julie had remembered the engagement or if the day's events had blotted it from her memory as well. He stepped out of the office into the main room, pulling his mobile from his pocket.

"Have you remembered . . . ?" he began as soon as Julie picked up.

"Dinner tonight," she said. "Your new sergeant and his wife . . . Yes, I thought of it after I dropped Richard at Fleet station. It's in the oven."

"Well done. I'd forgotten all about it. And I've now got a new inspector as well — a woman — so you'd better set an extra place."

He rang off quickly, before Julie could bombard him with the questions he knew he had just triggered, and re-joined Dorothy in his office.

"You probably gathered that John's coming to mine for dinner," he said.

She nodded, smiling. "Which you'd forgotten."

"Well, er, yes, but you're invited too. It's all fixed."

Nonplussed, Dorothy pointed out that there was hardly time for her to drive home, get ready and return by seven o'clock. As a stranger to the area, she would probably also have trouble finding Blade's home in the dark. The weather could also be a problem and the roads might be icy . . . But he brushed all her excuses aside.

"There's no need to get changed. Follow me home, so you'll know where I live. And in the unlikely event of us being snowed in, we have a spare room. In light of what I've been telling you, it will be a good opportunity for you to make your own assessment of Julie. You, John and I will also have the chance to get to know each other properly. From what I've seen so far, I think we'll make a good team."

Not entirely reluctantly, Dorothy abandoned her plan for a takeaway in front of a cosy fire.

* * *

Despite their misgivings, Julie and Dorothy took to each other immediately. While Dorothy was freshening up in the bathroom, Blade told his wife that he had confided the whole story in her. So, when Dorothy came down to the kitchen and offered to help, Julie found it a relief to be able to talk about her worries and fears to someone other than her husband.

The arrival of the Hydes, who were in blissful ignorance of their hosts' problems, heralded a change to more light-hearted topics of conversation, and the evening proved to be a great success.

Becky turned out to be a surprise, quite different from what the others had imagined. Next to Hyde's lanky height, her diminutive figure looked almost comical, and they made an ill-matched couple. However, her lively personality quickly destroyed this first impression. A round face, framed by unruly, frizzy golden hair was saved from plainness by large, soft green eyes and a wide smile. She wasn't shy, nor was she intimidated by the seniority of the rest of the company. Unafraid, she aired her opinions on everything from politics to pop and films to fashion, and her remarks were far from unintelligent. Her new husband, who sat opposite her at the table, gazed at her with undisguised pride.

After the meal, the three women settled comfortably around the open fire, the coffee pot between them. Dorothy and Becky would be driving, so they had each limited themselves to one glass of wine during dinner, just enough to loosen their tongues on the subject of their husbands' stubborn ways and lack of common sense. Dorothy told them about Bramshill's spooky inhabitant, causing much merriment with the tale of the White Lady and John Hyde's assertion that there was no such thing as ghosts.

Blade and his sergeant remained seated at the table, whisky bottle between them, to discuss their plans for tomorrow. But Hyde's heart obviously wasn't in it. He kept glancing at the women, who at one point were all looking straight at him and giggling.

Blade misread his companion's unease as tiredness and gave up on the idea of drawing up a battle plan.

"Come on, John, it's time to call it a day." He rose to his feet. "Sorry, ladies. Bedtime. It's an early start tomorrow."

"I don't care how early it is," Becky replied defiantly, looking steadily at Blade, "I'll still make sure my husband leaves with a good breakfast inside him."

"We've been hearing how jealous you were this morning," Dorothy said, grinning at her boss.

"But you needn't think I'm getting up early to cook for *you*," added Julie. "I've told Becky that she'll soon learn." Then, in an aside to Dorothy, "Would you rise before dawn to feed your husband? Or perhaps it's the other way around and he knows how to boil a kettle and poach an egg. You must both work unsocial hours."

"Husband?" Blade joined in, embarrassed. "I'm sorry, I hadn't realised . . . well, I noticed the ring, of course, but I just didn't think. I shouldn't have hijacked you for the evening the way I did. Your husband would have been very welcome too, of course. If only I'd thought . . ."

Dorothy laughed. "Don't worry, he's not all alone at home. He left this morning for Brussels — a two-day conference — and goodness knows where he'll go when that's finished. He's a journalist on the *Record*."

Blade's jaw dropped and he stared at her in dismay. So, his inspector was married to a Fleet Street red-top reporter. What would she have been telling him?

"Ee, your face! It's a picture," she chuckled, her Geordie accent suddenly reasserting itself. "But there's no danger of me telling him any police secrets. When we first met I was a WPC and he was a reporter on the *Shields Gazette* — which I'll have you know is the oldest evening newspaper in the country — and we came to an agreement that we've stuck to ever since. He doesn't tell me about stories that might be spoilt if the police got wind of them, and I don't give him tips about police activity."

Becky broke the awkward silence that followed by thanking their hosts for a delightful evening and praising Julie's cooking. Her final comment — "I think we three wives have bonded really well, and it's been fun" — brought on another fit of the giggles.

Outside, the cold sent the departing guests scurrying for their cars. It had been snowing, depositing a light dusting on the car windscreens that was now beginning to freeze.

Dorothy was away first, the wheels of her Renault Mégane spinning wildly before the tyres found an unreliable grip. She had travelled barely half a mile before she noted the time on the dashboard clock: just turned half past ten. Not too late. She pulled into a lay-by and made a lengthy call to Chief Superintendent Stanley Oliver.

Becky turned the key three times before their car started. Their breath, twin clouds of vapour, was already misting the windows, and the heater fan was sending out a blast of arctic air. She rubbed the windscreen with her gloved hand.

"What are we waiting for?" he asked.

"I'm nervous. I've never driven on snow and ice before, and we're steaming up," she complained. "How long does it take for the engine to warm up and work the heater?"

"Not long. You'll be okay. Just take it easy."

She switched on the wipers, which made matters worse, since they too had frozen. She put the car into gear and they crawled out of the drive.

Becky drove carefully, until Hyde broke the silence. "You shouldn't have told them what the boss said about my breakfast. He'll think I've been moaning."

"Go on. They all thought it was funny."

"And why were you all laughing at me?"

"That was it. The breakfast."

"It wasn't that funny," he muttered.

Becky drove on for a while, and then said crossly, "Let's see if you think it's funny when I don't cook your bloody breakfast in the morning."

Hyde made no reply. She shot a quick, angry look at him.

He was asleep.

CHAPTER SIX

THE INCIDENT room was buzzing. Everyone, aware that Blade was keen for an early start, had arrived before seven and had already been assigned their tasks for the day.

Adrian Harper and Lucy Ramsay were to continue, and hopefully finish, their checks on the Syndicate Six students. Dorothy was due to see the landlord of the King's Head, and John Hyde would accompany Blade to interview Inspector Angela Liddell after they had spoken to Roger Cotter, the security manager.

"Bill, you can sit in on that," Blade said. "Cotter might tell us something that you and Tony Robinson could follow up. I still have a gut feeling that CCTV has a strong bearing on this case."

Bill Headley and Anthony Robinson both nodded. Blade turned to Dorothy. "Later, when you've finished at the King's Head and I've seen Angela Liddell, you and I can take a trip up to London to see Ashington's widow." He glanced at Hyde. "I assume she's been told?"

"Yeah, the Met's dealt with that. The commandant contacted them straight away."

"Good. We can go and see her then, Dorothy. After all, the wife is usually the prime suspect. John, you could travel up with us and visit the Yard. Have a nose around, see what you can dig out. It wouldn't surprise me if Ashington had a few enemies up there."

Back in the incident room, Blade looked at his watch. "I thought this man Cotter is always in by seven thirty. It's twenty to eight now, so where the hell is he?"

"Maybe the weather has delayed him," suggested the sergeant.

"Well, *we've* all managed to get in, no problem. Bill, ring security and check," Blade said impatiently. He turned to Hyde. "So, did you have a good breakfast?"

"No. Cornflakes. Becky didn't get up," Hyde muttered.

Blade couldn't hide his smile. "A quick learner, your Becky."

"She seems to think I've done something wrong, but I don't know what it is, and she won't say."

"Ah, that's women for you," Blade said sagely.

Headley returned. "Sir, Mr Cotter is in. He arrived spot on seven thirty and is aware that you want to see him. Apparently, he'd hardly sat down before his desk phone rang. He picked it up, listened briefly, and dashed out without a word. The bloke I spoke to thought he must have come here."

"Well, he hasn't," Blade said. "What the devil is he playing at? Bring him to me the minute he gets here," he added to Hyde and stomped off to his office.

Hyde nodded and turned to look at the whiteboard. Stroking his chin thoughtfully, he studied the photograph of Inspector Angela Liddell that he had pinned up the previous afternoon. He remembered the deputy commandant describing her as being very fit and into karate. She gave the impression of being strong. With her dark hair pinned up in a bun under her hat and the unsmiling mouth and expressionless eyes, the official portrait gave no clue as to her character. Hyde speculated that, given her connection to Ashington, she must surely also rank as a prime suspect.

A loud shout, almost a screech, caused him to spin around. A woman stood in the open doorway. Wearing running shorts and top, she was leaning slightly forward and breathing heavily. Her face, arms and legs were red with cold, and her right hand was raised, pointing straight at the astonished detective sergeant.

"I'm sorry, miss, you're not allowed in—"

Still panting, she demanded, "What's . . . my . . . bloody . . . picture . . . doing . . . up . . . there?"

Hyde realised that she was pointing, not at him, but at the board behind him. With the dark, almost jet black hair now wet with snow and hanging in strings about her shoulders, she bore little resemblance to the photograph.

"Ah, Inspector Angela Liddell, I presume," said Blade, who had come to see what the noise was about. "Do come in. As it happens, I want to see you about—"

"And I want to see you," she broke in angrily. "I've come to report that there's a dead man in my room."

After a short, stunned silence, Blade asked, "Do you know the man?"

"Yes, of course I bloody know him, everyone here does. He's always prowling about the place. He's the security chief. I think his name's Cotter."

* * *

Angela Liddell, still red-faced — not with cold now, but with anger — was huddled in a luxurious soft white dressing gown belonging to Felicity Dumble. It did nothing to improve her mood, nor did the comfortable chesterfield in the deputy commandant's suite.

She was furious because Blade had refused to allow her to return to her room to get dressed.

Mrs Dumble tried to placate her. "Well, I'm sure you know he's right. He can't let you go back to your room. It's a crime scene. But as soon as forensics have finished in there, he'll have your gear transferred to your new place. I've already arranged for you to move into a room a few doors down the corridor. Lucky really, we don't usually have vacancies, but some courses have been discontinued ahead of the college closure, so there's plenty of available rooms."

"That's all very well, but I'm supposed to be at a lecture at nine o'clock and I can hardly turn up in your dressing gown."

Felicity smiled. "Agreed — and I'm sorry I can't lend you some clothes, you're quite a bit bigger than me and you'd never get into them. You're welcome to the dressing gown, though, and you can stay here for as long as necessary. Anyway, Superintendent Blade said he'd be along to see you as soon as he's finished with the pathologist, and he wouldn't be at all happy to find you gone." She looked at her watch. "But now there's a lecture *I* must attend. I'm giving it!"

* * *

Fred Stoker grinned. "You're keeping me busy, Ralph. Two murders in two days. They'll be renaming the place Midsomer Bramshill."

"It *is* murder then?" Blade said.

The pathologist nodded. "I'm sure of it. It's just like yesterday — cyanide. The same smell of almonds and no sign of either the drinking vessel or the poison's container. Whoever's responsible has cleared up. As you can see, it looks as if the victim — I understand he's the head of security here — swallowed the stuff, fell forward and was just left where he landed."

The two men were standing in the doorway of Angela Liddell's room. As well as a single bed and bedside table, the plain but serviceable furniture comprised a wardrobe, a small chest of drawers and a wooden chair pushed under a desk with a hinged lid over its storage compartment. A bucket armchair provided the sole, forlorn attempt at comfort. There was one window above the single radiator. On the far side of the room an open door revealed an en suite containing a bath with a shower over it, a washbasin and toilet.

Hanging outside the wardrobe was the uniform of a woman police inspector. A crisp white shirt, navy pullover, undergarments, stockings and a clip-on black tie were all draped over the wooden chair. Underneath, a pair of shiny black shoes mirrored the light. On top of the chest of drawers sat a silver-framed photograph of Angela Liddell with an older woman who, Blade guessed, was her mother. On the bedside table a lamp, a telephone and a book, with a bookmark sticking out, were the only things on view.

All neat and tidy. Everything had its place.

Everything but Roger Cotter's body.

Lying face down on the wood block floor, this ugly, chilling proof of violent disorder destroyed all illusion of calmness and order. The head was twisted to the left, slightly raised by the fingers of the left hand, which were frozen in the act of clawing the neck, just under the chin. Etched on his contorted face, a mixture of fear and pain recorded the dying seconds of the security manager's life.

"Poor devil," muttered Stoker. Then, more loudly, indicating the white-clad forensics team members who were still busy taking photographs and dusting for fingerprints. "They'll be finished with him soon and I can get him to the lab. I'll let you know as soon as I find anything."

He smiled grimly. "At least you won't be asking me the usual question: time of death."

"Thanks, Fred." Blade turned to leave, and then paused to study the layout of the accommodation block. They were on the ground floor, with rooms on each side of a broad corridor. Angela Liddell's room was just four doors away from Felicity Dumble's suite, which was at the end of the passage and, he noted with a wry smile, directly opposite the commandant's quarters.

He changed his mind about leaving, retraced his steps and called Hyde on his mobile.

"John, we'll do the Liddell interview now. You know where she is. I'll see you there."

* * *

Angela Liddell sat stiffly to attention on the chesterfield, feet planted firmly on the floor, striving to retain some measure of dignity. The borrowed dressing gown made her feel vulnerable and self-conscious, almost naked. The two detectives, seated on chairs they had carried across from the dining table, looked down on her.

Her discomfort increased under Blade's silent stare of appraisal, while Hyde fiddled with his notebook and scribbled with his pen, getting the ink to flow. Her earlier resentment had given way to an increasing feeling of apprehension and an unnatural pallor had replaced the angry red flush on her cheeks. The continued silence prompted an urgent need to fill it. Finally, she capitulated and burst out with, "Why is my picture on your board?"

"I'll ask the questions, Inspector," said Blade. "Why was Mr Cotter in your room?"

"I . . . I've no idea. He was there when I got back from my run."

"How did he get in?"

She shrugged. "I don't know. I could hardly ask him, could I? Perhaps he just opened the door and walked in."

"Don't try to be clever with me."

She shook her head. "I'm not trying to be clever. The door wasn't locked. I was only going to be out an hour at the most, and as this place is full of coppers, I thought it ought to be safe enough. Anyway, there are no pockets in my running gear to carry a key."

"What time did you leave your room?"

"Seven. Same as every morning."

"Did anyone see you?"

She said nothing for a few moments. "Why are you treating me like this, like some . . . some criminal? You're acting as though you think *I* killed him."

John Hyde leaned forward, staring at her. "Well, did you?"

"No, of course I didn't!"

"You do know why we're here, Miss Liddell?" Blade added. "Here at Bramshill?"

She nodded.

"Well, look at it from our point of view. Chief Superintendent Harold Ashington who, we're told, you accused of sexual assault, has been murdered. He, in case you didn't know, denied any such thing and claimed it was the other way around, that *you* attacked *him* when he rebuffed your advances. He said you stabbed him with a pair of nail scissors before he escaped. Which is consistent with a wound that was found during the post-mortem examination."

"So that answers your question doesn't it?" Hyde said. "Your picture is on the board because you have a close link with the victim."

"And then," Blade resumed, "lo and behold, an important witness we were waiting to interview turns up dead. In your room. What are we supposed to think?"

Her pallor now matched the colour of the borrowed dressing gown. "Shouldn't this interview be taking place in the police station?" she asked shakily.

"No, you're not under arrest and we're not charging you — yet. But, as they say in the movies, don't leave town. Now, can I have an answer please. Did anyone see you leave for your run at seven o'clock?"

"Yes, the commandant. He was passing my room as I came out and he remarked on the weather. There was a car waiting outside and the driver opened the door for him, so he must have seen me set off. As I began my run the car went past, heading for the drive. I didn't see anyone else, it had started to snow quite heavily, until the end of the run, when I saw a few people hurrying to and from the dining room. They were muffled up, so I didn't recognise any of them."

Blade pulled his mobile from his pocket, switched off *Für Elise* in mid-rendition and went out into the corridor to take the call. He was back within a minute.

"We'll have to go," he said hurriedly to his sergeant. He turned to Angela. "We'll need to talk to you again. Your clothes will be brought to you soon, but I suggest you wait here until Mrs Dumble gets back. She will take you to your new room."

Outside, he said, "That was Dorothy on the phone. Forensics have just called to say that they've found a flask containing whisky. They've sent it for analysis but are pretty sure there's cyanide mixed with it."

Hyde whistled softly. "Where did they find it?"

"In Angela Liddell's chest of drawers, hidden among her underwear."

CHAPTER SEVEN

BLADE CALLED a quick conference to bring the team up to date, amend the programme for the day, hear reports and share ideas. Hyde didn't attend. He was busy arranging meetings in London — one, for himself, at Scotland Yard and another, for the superintendent and Dorothy with Ashington's widow. He had a civilian driver standing by to take them to Reading station. To Hyde's delight Blade had insisted on a faster, main line train to Paddington so they could get refreshments, doubting that the local Fleet-Waterloo trains had buffet cars.

"Lucy, have you turned up anything interesting among the Syndicate Six students?" Blade asked.

"Not so far, sir. We've interviewed them all. They, er, they're all chief supers and they don't seem very happy at being questioned by constables, but they all say they got on well enough with Mr Ashington and none of them knew him before meeting him on this course. We're contacting their home forces for background and history checks, but that's even more, um, awkward, sir, because then we'll be dealing with people who are even more senior."

Blade tried to hide a smile. "Don't let them wear you down. Carry on with the good work, but you'll have to do it on your own, I'm afraid, because," He shifted his gaze to Harper. "Adrian, I'm putting you on nights. We've had two murders already, so I think we should have a permanent presence here. You can keep an eye on things, do the odd patrol — see that Inspector Liddell doesn't do a runner, for instance. Apart from her room, and the commandant and his deputy's quarters at the other end of the corridor, that block is empty because student numbers are down now the college is closing. I'll get the accommodation people to fix up a room for you near Liddell's, so you can rest now and then." He grinned. "And if any of Bramshill's famous ghosts venture out tonight, I reckon *you* will scare *them*. You'd better go home now, have a sleep and be back here at seven. I'll see you then."

"Yes, sir!" Adrian rose, his chair grating noisily against the wood block floor. He directed a nod and a fleeting smile at Lucy Ramsay, who watched him go, unable to disguise her disappointment.

"Which brings us back to the CCTV cameras," Blade said. "It seems strange that Mr Cotter, the man who might have been able to tell us something, and the very person we've been waiting to speak to, is murdered as soon as he gets back. Bill, Tony, I want you to dig deep into the backgrounds of Cotter and all his staff. See if there's any connection between them, apart from being work colleagues. Check his desk phone. Find out where that call came from this morning before he hurried out. And I also want to know if there's a link between Cotter and the first victim, Ashington. Go over that film again, very slowly, and—"

"We're already on to it, sir," Bill Headley broke in. "As you'd expect, none of the security staff have a criminal record. But as for the film, when we heard yesterday that the time of Ashington's death was earlier than thought, we had another look, going right back to one pm. Tony?"

Tony Robinson read from his notebook:

"At seven minutes and fifteen seconds past two the screen froze for almost two minutes, until eight minutes and twelve seconds past two. After that, everything was normal until it froze again that night between ten fifty and nine seconds and ten fifty-four precisely."

Headley resumed. "It was difficult to spot until we slowed the film because, oddly, there was nobody about and there was no movement in the hall both times it froze and restarted — which was natural in the mansion at night, but unusual in the afternoon, when staff are coming and going. Now that Mr Cotter can't help us, sir, I've arranged for someone from the firm that installed the CCTV to come in."

Blade beamed at them. "Well done, you two. That's very good work. I want it all written up and on my desk by the time I get back from London."

He rose just as Hyde entered the room. "Come on, Dorothy. Time we were out of here."

* * *

The train was crowded when they at boarded at Reading, so the three detectives found a quiet spot in a first class carriage where they could discuss the case without being overheard. There was a buffet car attached to the train, so Hyde volunteered to fetch coffee and sandwiches. When the sergeant — still grinning at his chief's quip about being fixated on food because Becky hadn't cooked his breakfast — had gone, Blade asked Dorothy about her visit to Gerald Harptree, the landlord of the King's Head.

"Nothing new," she said. "He corroborated exactly what your son Richard told you." She bit her lip, an anxious frown creasing her brow. "Look, sir, you know the chief super has confirmed everything you told me yesterday and I'm with you all the way, but . . . but I really think I should interview Richard myself, for my own satisfaction, to . . . to be sure that there's nothing . . ."

"To convince yourself that he's telling the truth and isn't a killer," Blade finished for her.

"Well . . ." She shrugged and gave a rueful smile.

"Yeah, I can understand that, so go ahead. I'll warn him to expect you sometime and to co-operate."

"And I also think," she charged on bravely, "that you should tell John Hyde everything. He's a good lad, and I think you'll find he'll be onside. Anyway, it's all bound to come out eventually, and if you keep him in the dark, he'll think you don't trust him, which is not good for a key member of your team."

Blade drew a deep breath and sat silently for a while, thinking. Then he nodded. "Okay. You tell him."

He stood up as the door at the end of the carriage slid open to admit the sergeant, who was struggling to keep a laden tray level. Concentrating hard, eyes fixed on the tray, he teetered towards them. His smile of triumph was just a split second premature. As he leaned to set it down, a particularly vicious jerk made him lurch forward, the tray landed heavily on the table, and the coffee slopped over.

"Oh, sh— Sorry."

Dorothy immediately snatched up the sandwiches, coffee and other items and transferred them to the table. The men stood by awkwardly.

"Sorry about that," Hyde said lamely.

The three detectives regarded the liquid sloshing from side to side in the plastic tray. Blade picked it up. "I'm going for a pee. I'll take this with me and get it dried." He looked at Dorothy. "You might as well tell him now."

"Tell me what?" Hyde asked. Blade was already going through the sliding door.

"Sit beside me, have a sandwich and what's left of the coffee, and I'll tell you," Dorothy said.

It took ten minutes of fast talking to explain Ralph Blade's involvement with Harold Ashington, her original doubts, her assurances from Chief Superintendent Stanley Oliver and to answer the young sergeant's own questions.

When Blade returned with a dry tray, blaming "a queue at the loo" for his lengthy absence, Hyde was sitting deep in thought.

"Well, what's the verdict, John?"

"I'm glad I've been told, sir, pleased you feel you can rely on me. I trust DI Fraser's judgement, so if it's good enough for her, it's fine with me. I'll be happy to give you my full support — but I don't think the rest of the team should know. They may not all feel the same and it could derail the investigation."

"Ee, pet, you can call me Dorothy when it's just the three of us."

Hyde grinned, noting for the first time that she could switch the Geordie accent on and off to suit the occasion.

"Thank you, ma'am — er, Dorothy."

"And thank you both for your confidence in me," Blade added. "Now, let's pool our thoughts. We've got not one, but two murders to solve. Your thoughts, John?"

"Well, the murders must surely be linked, boss, and, to me, the common denominator is Inspector Angela Liddell. We know she was involved with Ashington — she even stabbed him with a pair of scissors. And Cotter's body was found, of all places, in her room. Both victims had been poisoned with cyanide. And where was a flask of whisky-cyanide toddy discovered? In her room, hidden in her knickers!"

A smile flickered across Blade's lips. "The cyanide mixture isn't confirmed yet."

"And why would she be so silly as to leave it there?" Dorothy wondered. "She could easily have emptied the flask, wiped it clean, and binned it somewhere, maybe on her way across to the mansion to report 'finding' the body in her room."

"And she wouldn't have had time to get rid of *that*," Blade said. "But what was Cotter doing in her room anyway?"

"They were obviously involved," Hyde said. "He knew we wanted to interview him, so he dashed over to ask her what to say. Erm . . ." He stroked his chin. "Let's suppose Cotter had been getting his leg over, Ashington found out and was threatening to expose them — you say that's the way he operated, boss. Maybe Cotter and Liddell disagreed about what to tell us. He might have wanted to tell the truth and come clean about their affair, so she gave him a swig of whisky to 'calm his nerves' — and shut him up for good."

Dorothy shook her head. "He wouldn't be daft enough to accept a drink from her, knowing—"

"He probably didn't know the cause of death," Hyde cut in, "or even that she might have actually killed Ashington. Don't forget, Cotter'd been away, fishing. When he arrived this morning, his staff would have given him the news of the murder and said we wanted to speak to him. What's the first thing he does? He dashes off to see Angela and find out if we know about them and their involvement with Ashington."

"I don't buy that," Dorothy said. "She wouldn't take the risk. Liddell knows how the police work. Before her promotion to inspector she did five years in CID, the last two as a sergeant. I looked up her record. She's hell bent on climbing the career ladder."

The train shuddered and creaked. They had started the long crawl into Paddington.

"Here we are then," said Blade, standing to drag his coat down from the rack. "John, when you get to the Yard, ask for Superintendent Jack Wriggley. He's an old mate. I've had a word with him, and he'll point you towards people who knew Chief Superintendent Ashington really well, those who worked with him or knew him socially. Dig hard, you might find someone who disliked him enough to murder him."

They edged towards the exit, joining the knot of passengers ready to leave. Nobody talked. In the strange, almost breathless silence, all eyes seemed to be fixed intently on the window, watching, waiting. When the train finally came to a halt it was so gentle it took a split second to register that the door was open. The race was on. The horde spilled onto the platform. Some hurried to the Underground station to be squeezed into another hot and airless train, some to be first in the queue for taxis while others, bundled out of the main stream, paused to look around with worried expressions, wondering which way to go. This was London.

The three detectives took their time as they headed for the Circle line, where they parted company to travel in opposite directions — Blade and Dorothy heading for King's Cross, from where they would catch another tube to Finsbury Park. John Hyde went on to St James's Park, the closer station to Scotland Yard. They planned to meet up again at Paddington for the six thirty train back to Reading.

CHAPTER EIGHT

BLADE SET a brisk pace up Gillespie Road. There was no sign of snow here, but a zigzag of weak yellow sunshine that was trying to force a way through the cloud cover did nothing to raise the near freezing temperature. It gave up the fight and retreated before they had gone a hundred yards.

Dorothy turned up the collar of her parka and pulled a bright red woolly hat down over her ears. She wasn't looking forward to questioning a newly widowed woman. She guessed that Blade didn't fancy it either, which was why he had brought her along. She shot a resentful glare in his direction.

"Is it far?"

"Six or seven minutes," he answered tersely, looking all around. Dorothy wondered if perhaps he was remembering the days — and nights — when as a young bobby on the beat he had patrolled these very streets. They walked on in silence.

At the end of Gillespie Road, they turned left and then immediately right. "Nearly there," said Blade. The neat nameplate read Herrick Road N5.

"Oh, wow! This is posh." She came to an abrupt halt and her eyes widened with pleasure. The trees lining the street were forlorn now, raising bare, twisted arms in supplication for an end to this dreary winter. Even so, many of the small gardens were half-hidden in neatly trimmed evergreen hedgerows.

But it was the elegant Victorian terrace that stole the show, its ornately bay-fronted homes immaculate. All had white window frames but the shiny front doors were painted in a variety of colours.

Blade spun around to face her. "Yeah, very posh. You could have one of these — if you happened to have a spare million or two."

"Being a chief super at the Yard must be a pretty good number," Dorothy said.

He grinned. "Maybe, but I don't think it's *that* good. Come on, it's time for us to meet the grieving widow."

Blade pulled a piece of paper from his pocket and strode on for about fifty yards before stopping again. "This is it."

She followed him up the short path and stood behind him while he rang the bell. They waited. Blade raised his hand to ring again when the door opened just wide enough for them to view half a face. Framed by curly red hair, one clear green eye peered out at them.

"Yes?"

Blade stepped aside, gesturing for Dorothy to move forward.

"Mrs Ashington? Good afternoon. I'm Detective Inspector Fraser." She held up her warrant card. "And this is Detective Superintendent Blade, of Hampshire Police. We're here to—"

"Oh!" The door opened wide. "That was quick. I knew you were coming, but I thought it would take you at least another hour. Come in, come in. I'll put the kettle on. You'll be ready for a cuppa after your journey. And I made a chocolate cake and some scones this morning. Do you like chocolate cake? I'll warm the scones, they'll be nice with strawberry jam and cream."

Sylvia Ashington ushered the visitors in and took their coats, smiling broadly and chattering non-stop, as if she felt under some compulsion to talk. "It's bitterly cold out, isn't it? Make yourselves comfortable, find somewhere to sit, first door on the right. I'll be along with the tea in a minute."

Dorothy, whose offer to help had been declined, was finding it difficult to disguise her bewilderment. Besides the effusive welcome, Sylvia herself was a surprise, nothing like she expected Ashington's widow to be. Plump, she thought charitably. Her round face was unlined, apart from an incipient double chin, and the vivid red of her mop of tight ginger curls looked entirely natural. Her make-up was minimal, because nothing could veil the freckles that swathed her cheeks and the snub nose that Sylvia thought of as blemishes. Perfect white teeth tended to draw attention away from them so, when she wasn't talking, she smiled a lot. Her clothes, elegant and obviously expensive, were another distraction. She was wearing a well-cut green tweed skirt with a cream V-neck cashmere cardigan, probably carefully chosen to emphasise the colour of her eyes. Dorothy guessed that the pearls around her neck and decorating her ears were genuine.

Dorothy tilted her head towards the kitchen, from where the chink of crockery could be heard. She went and stood beside her boss and whispered, "No widow's weeds here then."

He shook his head. "More like a merry widow."

Dorothy added, "We'd better do what she said, sit down and make ourselves comfortable." There were two armchairs and two three-seater settees, all of these covered in a deep cream fabric with a pattern of large, leafy red and white roses.

They chose a settee and sat down at each end. Dorothy looked up at the ceiling to admire the ornate plaster cornices and decorative centrepiece. Candelabra — at each end of the room — were already lit, repelling the outside winter gloom. There was no fire in the tiled Victorian fireplace, but the room was not cold. Modern central heating radiators, the television and a deep pile fitted carpet were the only slightly jarring features. The rest of the furniture was period — even the pictures on the walls.

At a sound from the doorway, they started to rise to their feet. Mrs Ashington pushed a tea trolley in and parked it beside the detective superintendent.

"No, don't get up." She walked quickly across to a nest of tables and carried one across to place between her visitors. "Help yourself to the scones and jam," she ordered Blade as she poured his tea, "then slide the trolley along to your colleague."

She smiled at Dorothy. "So, what do you think? I saw you looking around."

"Me? Ee!" Dorothy was taken unawares. "Oh, er, I think you have a remarkable home, Mrs Ashington. It's lovely"

The smile widened. "I'm glad you like it. But I'll tell you this: if *he'd* had his way, the house would have been ruined."

Puzzled, Dorothy's brow wrinkled. "Do you mean your husband, Mr Ashington? Really? How?"

"As soon as we were married, he wanted to rip the place apart and modernise it. You know – featureless. Plain ceilings, no fireplaces or period pieces. Just that horrid modern furniture. But I wasn't having any of it."

Blade leaned forward. "So, this house belongs to you, Mrs Ashington, not to your husband?"

"Yes, and please call me Sylvia. I'm going to drop my married name and revert to my maiden name, Lumley. I inherited the house when Dad died. I know he paid under ten thousand for it in the late sixties and — can you believe it? — a few weeks ago, a house just a few doors up the road went for nearly one and a half million!" The words continued to tumble out. "Of course, *you know who* had been trying for ages to get me to sell, hoping to get his hands on the cash. No way! But now I might just do that." She laughed. "You never know, you might see me on that TV programme, *Escape to the Country*. I could buy a really nice place and still have a tidy sum left over. I could even take Jack with me." She smirked. "Oh, yes, I've got a boyfriend. Right under his nose." She giggled. "One of his colleagues at the Yard too, and he never guessed. Serves the bastard right for the way he treated me all those years."

She paused briefly for breath. "And here's the funny thing, the icing on the cake. As the widow of a serving chief superintendent I'll get quite a hefty pension, won't I?"

"So long as you don't cohabit." Dorothy couldn't resist the remark. A glare from her boss silenced her.

Patting away some crumbs that had stuck to his chin, he said, "I'm sorry Mrs, er, Sylvia, we have nothing to do with pensions, although Detective Inspector Fraser and I are here in connection with your husband's death. I'm very sorry for your loss, but I'm afraid we must ask you some questions."

"Of course. I understand. I know why you're here." She smiled brightly. "You're investigating his murder. The spouse is always the prime suspect, isn't that right? So, ask away."

Dorothy pulled a notebook from her bag and began to take notes.

"Is there anyone you can think of who disliked your husband enough to want him dead?" Blade asked.

"Apart from me, do you mean?" Sylvia said. "I admit I hated the bugger enough, and I daresay there are quite a few others who are glad he's gone. I hope they never catch his killer because whoever they are did me a favour."

She paused and gazed steadily at her questioner. Her earlier lighthearted demeanour was gone and she continued slowly, enunciating each word.

"The only other person I can think of with a good enough reason to kill my husband is *you*."

"*Me*?" He and Dorothy stared at her, open mouthed.

"You said your name is Blade?"

He nodded.

"*Ralph* Blade?"

Again, a nod.

"There surely can't be two Ralph Blades on the force, so it must be you — and, boy, did he hate you! He couldn't stop ranting over how you pinched his girl . . . your wife, Julie. Then he'd start raving about how you'd stolen his son. He said he was going to get even with you and get his son back . . . because, you see, I couldn't," her voice faltered, "I couldn't . . ."

She waved away Dorothy's attempt to comfort her, dabbed her eyes with her paper napkin, took a deep breath and went on. "He said he'd have to get his son back because I couldn't give him one. The bastard kept taunting me, saying I wasn't a proper wife. He made me go to the doctor to find out why I couldn't conceive. I knew he'd been away to see his — *your* son. He meant to ruin your life. He planned to lure the boy — Richard? Is that his name? — away from you. And fool that he was, he even thought he could persuade Julie to leave you and go back to him. So I know you had a motive to kill him. I don't blame you, and I won't tell anyone."

Blade leaned forward, took her hand and said gently, "I didn't kill him, Sylvia, and I don't think you did either, but you'll have to make a formal statement. I'll make the arrangements and have a car sent for you."

Dorothy looked up from her notetaking. "Sylvia, how did you know what your husband was planning to do?"

"Because he told me, of course. The rotten sod didn't give a damn about me, about hurting me. I wanted children too, but he didn't think about how I felt. He just kept going on about it being all my fault."

Tears gone, a slow smile spread across her face. "You'll never believe the pleasure it gave me when I told him his plans had gone pear-shaped."

"How?" Blade asked. "How did they go pear-shaped? And when did you know?"

"Two days ago. Wednesday morning."

"That's the day he died," Blade said.

"Yes, that's right. Thank goodness he didn't die without knowing. That would've been a real let-down. But he knew all right. He didn't say anything, but he knew."

"Knew what?" Blade sounded exasperated. "He was in Bramshill on Wednesday. Were you there?"

"No. I had a call from the surgery that morning. Dr Mander, who's really nice, wanted to see me because he'd just

62

got the results of the tests and he had a ten-minute slot free at eleven fifteen, if I could make it. So, naturally I went along."

Blade glanced at Dorothy, trying to hide his exasperation.

"It wasn't me at all," Sylvia added triumphantly. "It was him all along. His sperm count was practically nil. So, you can tell your precious Julie that Harold couldn't have been Richard's father. All those years he blamed me for not having kids, when it was *his* fault. The bastard was firing blanks."

CHAPTER NINE

AT SCOTLAND Yard, John Hyde was shown up to the office of Superintendent Jack Wriggley, who was welcoming enough but seemed harassed and distracted.

"Ah, yes, Ralph Blade told me you were coming. How is my old mate? We used to be on the beat together not far from here, when we were young bobbies fresh out of Hendon. And now he's in charge of the investigation into the murder of Harold Ashington who, believe you me, was the bane of our lives back then." He paused. "So. Exactly what is it you're after?"

"Well, sir, we're putting together a profile of Mr Ashington. Detective Superintendent Blade is interviewing his wife as we speak to see if we can identify—"

"Yes, yes," Wriggley waved a hand. "Ralph did say something about that. I understand, but I don't really think I can help you. I didn't work with Ashington, you see, apart from those far-off days when I was a constable and he was a sergeant. When he was promoted, he was posted to a different station, so our paths never crossed."

He drummed his fingers on the desk. "Look, I'm very busy at the moment, getting ready for the move — you know the Yard is moving to the Victoria Embankment? — and things are a bit chaotic." He forced a laugh. "I don't know what the police service is coming to: forces merging, we're moving, Bramshill's closing altogether, not to mention the cuts. I think the best thing I can do for you is to put you in touch with someone from Ashington's department," he pulled his desk phone closer, "who worked with him and knew him well."

Hyde waited, listening to the loud burp-burp at the other end of the line. Wriggles, he thought sourly, was probably hoping to be in line for promotion, maybe to Ashington's job, and didn't want to get involved in case he put a foot wrong and scuppered his chances. The superintendent, his hand over the mouthpiece, smiled and mouthed something about taking a long time to answer. There was a click, and somebody said, "Spence."

"Ah, Sergeant. Superintendent Wriggley here. Can you pop up now? The visitor I spoke to you about earlier has arrived."

Hyde smiled to himself. So, you intended to dump me on to someone else all along.

* * *

Sergeant Jimmy Spence, dark, tall, lean and keen, breezed in, was introduced and ushered Hyde out of Wriggley's comfort zone. Safely out of earshot in the corridor he grinned. "I don't think his nibs is too happy about your visit. Internal politics and all that. Probably worried about saying the wrong thing. But I don't give a monkey's because I'm leaving soon, off to Avon and Somerset as an inspector."

"Congratulations. I'm sure you'll be happy there. It's a lovely part of the world."

"Yeah, thanks. Erm . . ." he chewed his lip and frowned. "I'm trying to think where we can talk without people earwigging while I dish the dirt on the late, unlamented Chief Superintendent Harold Ashington."

"Can we go and eat somewhere?" Hyde asked. "I'm bloody starving. I didn't get a proper breakfast, and I only had a sandwich on the train." He glanced at his watch and saw that it was just turned two thirty. "I suppose you've had lunch?"

Jimmy shook his head. "Nope. I've been stuck at my desk waiting for the call to meet you. We didn't know what time you were coming, and Wriggles would have had a fit if I wasn't there when he rang."

"Great! Lunch is on me. Where can we go?"

Jimmy's expression brightened. "The Feathers. It's only just up the road."

"Oh yeah, I saw it on my way in. Come on then."

They clattered down the stairs to the vestibule and were just about to exit when they were brought to a halt. "Sergeant Hyde!" Hyde turned to see Bramshill's commandant hurrying towards him, smiling broadly.

"You go on and grab a table," he said quickly to Spence. "I'll have to speak to this guy. I'll be with you as soon as I can."

"Fancy seeing you here," said the commandant, obviously unable to hide his curiosity as he watched Jimmy Spence go out to join the pedestrians in the Broadway. "So, what brings you to the Yard? Is it anything to do with this second murder? Terrible, terrible. I heard it was Roger Cotter. Is that right?"

"That's right, but I'm not here about that," Hyde said. He didn't elaborate. "I didn't expect to see you here, sir. I thought you said yesterday that you were going to the Home Office."

"Oh, I've been there. That was this morning. I've just been looking up old friends at the Yard. I used to work here you know. But I'm off to Bramshill now, and when I caught sight of you heading for the exit, I wondered if I might give you a lift." He raised his eyebrows.

"That's very kind of you, sir, but I haven't finished here yet, and I'm due to meet Detective Superintendent Blade and Detective Inspector Fraser at Paddington station later," said Hyde, again without explanation.

"Ah. A pity. It would have been nice to have had company . . . and a chat. You could have briefed me about poor Cotter's death."

"I probably don't know much more than you do, sir," Hyde said carefully. "We left for London fairly soon after it happened." A thought struck him. "If your car is here, sir, I'd like a word with your driver. He might have noticed something or someone out of the ordinary while he was waiting outside your place this morning. I remember you saying you were being picked up at seven." Another thought. "Or you, sir? Did you notice anything unusual?"

"Me? No. I went straight from my quarters to the car, quickly, because it was just starting to snow quite heavily. Oh — wait a minute — as I went down the corridor, Angela Liddell, the student we talked about at our meeting yesterday, came out of her room. She was dressed in running gear, but there was nothing unusual in that. She goes for a run at that time every morning, I think. We chatted about the weather until we parted at the entrance and I made a dash for the car. But you're right, you never know, the driver might have seen something. Come with me, and you can ask him."

* * *

After speaking to the driver, Hyde hurried down the road to the Feathers, where he stood just inside the door, taking in the wooden floor, brass fittings, panelling, mirrors and chandeliers. A real old Victorian pub. He spotted Jimmy Spence occupying a red leather seat in one of the booths, sipping beer and studying the menu. A full glass sat on the table.

"That's yours," said Jimmy. "The bangers and mash are very good here. So is the steak and ale pie with mashed potatoes and spinach, or the cod battered in ale with tartare sauce. But I think I'll have the grilled sea bass. A nice treat — seeing as how you're paying."

Hyde opted for the sausage and mash, wondering gloomily if Blade would allow him to put the bill on expenses. But the money he was laying out turned out to be well rewarded as the meal progressed and more pints were despatched, and his companion opened up about the gossip at Scotland Yard.

There were rumours, Jimmy confided, that Ashington's rise up the promotion ladder owed much to the fact that he "had something" on various senior officers.

"It's not just who you know but *what* you know," Jimmy added as he nudged his empty glass forward. "Anyway, who was that chap that nobbled you? I've seen him at the Yard quite a lot lately."

"Yeah, well, he used to be a chief superintendent there," Hyde said. "His name is Mr Roderick Chaytor-Gill, and he's the commandant at Bramshill."

"Ah, so that's the famous Chaytor-Gill. I've heard of him. He'll be redundant when Bramshill shuts, won't he, and word has it that he's the favourite for the post of Chief Inspector of Constabulary." He grinned. "So that's why he's been sniffing around here so much. Drumming up support. In his case I suppose it really is *who* you know."

With a glance at his watch, Hyde picked up his companion's glass. "Time for me to go and meet my boss. I'll pay the tab and get them to bring you another pint." He held out his free hand. "Nice to have met you, Jimmy. Good luck in your new job."

* * *

The three detectives were lucky on the train back to Reading. The rush hour was over and there were plenty of seats in first class where they could sit, huddled around the table, quietly exchanging the information they had gathered.

Blade was gratified to learn that his suspicion that Ashington had used blackmail to gain promotion was shared by others. He and Dorothy both seemed intrigued by Sergeant Hyde's encounter with the commandant.

Before the train reached Reading, Dorothy went to the toilet compartment, where she wouldn't be overheard, and spoke at length to her husband on her mobile.

"You've got contacts in the Home Office," she finished. "Find out all you can about Chaytor-Gill — but keep it under wraps. When it's time, I'll brief you and you'll be first with the news."

She ended the call and immediately made another, laughing with the woman who answered. "Stand by. It's tonight," she said, and hung up.

A car was waiting at the station to take them back to Bramshill, where they would collect their own vehicles. It was almost seven thirty when they arrived and the incident room was empty apart from PC Harper, who had reported for his first stint of night duty.

"Hello, Adrian," Blade said cheerily. All set then?"

"Sir," Harper said morosely.

Blade laughed. "That's the spirit. And talking of spirits, keep an eye open for those ghosts." He turned to his companions, adding, "See you in the morning. Early." And was gone.

As she and Hyde left the building, Dorothy paused and looked across at the mansion. "Hang on," she said. "Let's have a look at the scene-of-crime in the dark, while conditions are similar to when the body was placed in the chest. Something might occur to us."

"I doubt it," said Hyde. All he wanted was to get home to Becky, but Dorothy was already on the move. A sudden chill wind made flurries of snow dance in the light that shone over the steps up to the front door and he was glad to step into the warmth of the hall. They went across to the chest and stared inside.

"It all looks the same to me. Can we go now?"

She shook her head. "No. As we're here, we might as well go upstairs to the Long Gallery. That's supposed to be one of the White Lady's favourite, er, haunts. If we're lucky, we might see her. Come on."

Dorothy headed for the stairs, but Hyde stayed where he was.

"Oh, come on. You're not scared, are you? You're the one who says there's no such thing as ghosts."

Hyde stayed put.

"Move!" There was exasperation in her tone. "I might need you to protect me from the spirits. Follow me. That's an order you must obey because you're only a sergeant and I'm," she struggled to keep a straight face, "an in-spectre."

He groaned. "That's not at all funny." Reluctantly, he followed her up the stairs into the dimly lit Long Gallery, where she pushed him ahead with a hasty, "You go first."

They stood in silence for a few moments. "There you are," Hyde said. "Nothing. Can we go now — ma'am?"

"Yes, I suppose you're right. There's nothing here. Come on then."

Dorothy turned to go, but Hyde stayed rooted to the spot. The back of his neck prickled, and he felt sure his hair must be standing on end.

"Can you smell it?" he said in a hushed voice.

"Smell what?"

"The scent, the perfume. It's how she — the White Lady — announces her presence."

"Oh, very funny."

"But you must be able to smell it." He was almost pleading now, and there was a distinct tremor in his voice. "It's very strong."

"Oh, for heaven's sake, grow up, man. It's been a long day, and this isn't funny anymore." She glanced at her watch. "Hmm, nearly eight o'clock, which must be way past your bedtime, sonny. Come on."

This time he followed willingly, almost treading on her heels, until they were safely outside. They walked in silence to where their cars were parked.

"It really was strong," he said plaintively, breaking the silence. "The perfume. It really—"

"Don't be late tomorrow." She climbed into her car and drove off.

He watched until her taillights were smothered, first by the swirling white snowflakes and then by the black night lying in wait beyond.

* * *

"You look as though you've seen a ghost," Becky said to her husband when he walked into the living room.

"I think I might have," he replied wearily.

"Ah, busy day? You poor thing."

She hurried across to give him a hug and a kiss, but stood back. She pushed him away. The welcoming smile was gone, her expression now as bleak and unfriendly as the weather outside.

"Where have you been? And who with?" she demanded.

He shrugged, puzzled. "You know where."

"Don't play the innocent with me," Becky raged. "Who with? I said. I can smell her. You stink of her perfume."

The perfume! Hope began to dawn. Perhaps, at last, someone would listen to him.

"You can smell it too," he said the relief evident in his voice. The perfume, remember? It's the way the White Lady announces her presence—"

"Oh, give me strength! Do you think I'm stupid? Do you really expect me to believe that a ghost sprinkled you with scent, a day after you'd lectured us all, telling us that ghosts don't exist?"

The tenuous flicker of hope was snuffed out as Becky stormed from the room. What a day. No breakfast. And now it seemed an evening meal would be off the menu as well. Hyde was beginning to wonder if marriage was all it was cracked up to be. He sat for a few minutes, wondering what to do, then decided to find her and try to calm her down. When he left the room, he could hear her voice. She was laughing.

He found her in the kitchen with her mobile to her ear and still laughing. "Oh, here he is now. I think I'd better put him out of his misery. We'll talk again tomorrow."

"Who was that?" he asked.

"Dorothy."

"As in DI Fraser?"

"The same. You were set up, John boy. That's what we were all giggling about last night. You were so sure there was no such things as ghosts, that we decided to teach you a lesson. It was Dorothy's idea really. She said she'd lure you up to the Long Gallery and spray her perfume over the collar of your jacket. Then, when you arrived home, I could give you hell. Good, eh?"

"Well, I don't think it's funny."

"Oh, don't be such a misery. Consider it an extra punishment."

"Punishment?" Hyde was having trouble keeping up.

"For making me drive home in the snow last night. I was terrified. And you . . . you just went to sleep. That did it. No way was I going to get up to cook your breakfast."

Light dawned. "So that's what it was all about. Er, does that mean there's no evening meal either?"

Becky smiled. "It's in the oven. By the time you've washed and changed, it'll be on the table."

Later, in the bathroom, and later still, he decided there was quite a lot to be said for marriage after all.

* * *

Blade bought a bottle of champagne on the way home. Popping the cork, he told Julie the details of his encounters with Sylvia Ashington and her doctor, Michael Mander.

"The doc wasn't keen to talk at first, but when he knew that Sylvia had already spilled the beans — and his patient was dead anyway — he realised there was no point in keeping confidentiality and confirmed what Sylvia had said. There is no way Ashington could be Richard's father." He leaned back in his chair, smiling in comfortable satisfaction. "So now we can resume our normal happy family life, which might turn out to be even better than before, now that Ashington's not around to spoil it."

Julie's face clouded. "Do you really think so? Well, I hope you're right, but I can't help worrying that things will never be the same as they were. I phoned Richard today, straight after you rang to tell me the good news. He was over the moon, of course, but he's still resentful about the way you spoke to him. He described you as a bullying cop and he still thinks you don't trust him."

"Why should he think that? Surely, he can see that I had to get to the bottom of what was going on. What was I supposed to think when it came out that he was meeting that bloody man behind our backs."

Julie pulled a face. "Look at it from Richard's point of view. After the poor boy was suddenly confronted with the possibility that a new acquaintance might in fact be his father, he told you that whatever happened, you would still be his dad. I heard him say it, in this very room. But *you* . . . you just went cold on him."

Blade opened his mouth to speak but she silenced him with a gesture. "You froze him out, at the very moment he needed you most. He was vulnerable and very scared. He'd just learned that the man he thought was a friend might *really* be his biological father. Then he finds out that this man has been murdered. And on top of that, *you*, the man best placed to help him," her voice cracked, "you tell him he could be the prime suspect and send him away. Alone. Was that the best you could come up with?"

She broke down in tears. Blade held her close. "The best I can do is find Ashington's killer," he said quietly. "Meantime I want to keep Richard out of the way for as long as possible. The last thing I want is for him to become a central part of the inquiry, or even get arrested. Maybe I was a bit hard on the lad, but I'll make it up to him." Thinking of Dorothy's remark on the train earlier in the day that 'for her own satisfaction' she should interview Richard herself, he added, "I'll ring him and give him some advice on how to handle any questions he might be asked. I know Dorothy wants to speak to him. But right now," he reached for the bottle, "let's finish this bubbly."

They clinked glasses, smiling at each other, but their celebration was muted. Blade could still sense his wife's resentment.

Could the family survive?

* * *

Dorothy arrived home cold and hungry. She hurried indoors, turned the heating up, put the kettle on to make tea, tipped the cod, chips and mushy peas she'd picked up at the takeaway onto a plate, and settled in front of the television to eat.

Two hours later, Bob Fraser found her curled up on the sofa, fast asleep. The weatherman was rounding off the ten o'clock news with dire warnings for the morning. Bob silenced him in mid-sentence and turned to look at his wife, enjoying the thrill he always felt when he looked at her. He knelt down beside her and stroked her cheek.

She stirred, opened one eye and yawned. "Oh, it's you. I was just dreaming that a handsome stranger was about to carry me off after saving me from a dreadful fate. Then I woke up and _you_ were there."

"Yeah. Me. And I'm going to carry you upstairs. But I'm no stranger."

"No." Dorothy studied his strong regular features, his smiling mouth, deep blue eyes and dark hair. "And not handsome either." She peered up at the clock on the mantelpiece. "But you're right about one thing. It's bedtime, so I'll let you carry me upstairs. We have to be up early in the morning."

"Well, you do," Bob smiled smugly. "It's my day off."

She punched his shoulder. "That's not fair. Can't you change it? Save it for when I'm free, so we can have some prime time together?"

"We can never guarantee when that will be. Anyway, I've got to go up to town to do some work for you. My Home Office contact has promised to see what he can dig out about the info you want, and I've arranged to meet him tomorrow afternoon."

He pulled her to her feet, swung her into his arms and carried her upstairs. Although only an inch taller than Dorothy, he made it look easy.

CHAPTER TEN

ADRIAN HARPER was bored. It was snowing hard outside, so he was damned if he was going to go out on patrol. It would be impossible to see anything anyway. What the hell was he expected to do? Sit outside Angela Liddell's next door-but-one room all night? It was all very well for Blade to say make sure she doesn't do a runner, but . . .

He checked his watch. Ten minutes past two on a cold, dark wintry morning. He had lost count of the times he'd opened the door of his room to peer down the corridor, but felt compelled to do it once more.

Nothing had changed. The dimly lit corridor remained empty, Angela's door firmly shut. The only excitement had happened at eleven thirty, when he had glimpsed a shadowy shape flit across the far end of the passage. In the gloom of the weak nightlights it was impossible to be sure but — Adrian smiled faintly at the memory —Roderick Chaytor-Gill seemed to be paying a visit to his deputy.

He closed the door and decided a cup of coffee would help him to stay awake. He'd had three already. As he filled the kettle in the bathroom, he blessed the staff who had prepared the room for him. A table had been set up with a plentiful supply of teabags, packets of coffee, a variety of biscuits, and a large jug of fresh milk. Even better than a hotel. A comfortable easy chair and a footstool with a cosy rug had also been brought in.

Gratefully, Adrian settled himself in the chair, feet up, with the rug arranged over his legs. Maybe this wasn't such a bad job after all.

He reached over for the steaming mug of coffee — and dropped it, spilling the contents over the floor. A piercing scream brought him to his feet. He hurried out into the corridor, untangling himself from the rug as he went.

This time Angela's door was open, and he ran in. There was no light on, but in the faint glow that leaked from the passage, he made out the figure of a hooded man wrestling on the bed with Angela, her face a blur of fear and pain as she struggled to get out from beneath him.

Adrian flung himself at her attacker, who grunted in surprise when the constable's bulk hit him. He released Angela and twisted around to fight him off. The hood of the man's anorak was hampering Adrian's attempt to wrap an arm around his neck until, suddenly, the battle was over. A flash of light coincided with a sickening thud. Adrian had a brief, frightening sensation that his head had exploded.

And then. Nothing.

* * *

Blade struggled from a deep sleep and fumbled for the bedside phone.

"Blade," he said, trying to stifle a yawn and watching Julie, who had just entered the bedroom.

"Chaytor-Gill here, Superintendent. I've just found a man — I think he's one of yours — in Inspector Liddell's room. He's unconscious and so is she. An ambulance is on its way."

Blade sat up, wide awake now. "I'll be there in ten minutes. I know I don't need to tell you not to touch anything, sir."

"Well, obviously, I've had to touch them to attend to them," he said testily. "And so has Mrs Dumble, who is here with me."

Blade hung up. "Got to go. Emergency," he said to Julie, who was climbing into bed beside him. "Are you just coming to bed?" He touched her cheek. "You're freezing. Are you all right?"

"Yes, I'm fine. Couldn't sleep, so I went down for a cup of tea. I didn't look at the time. What is it?"

"Three o'clock, the witching hour," he said, dressing hurriedly. "Try and get some shuteye. Move over to my side of the bed, I've warmed it for you."

The snow had stopped, and he drove fast, slipping and sliding along the deserted roads. As he turned into Bramshill's long drive an ambulance, approaching from the opposite direction, fell in behind him.

When both vehicles had parked outside the accommodation block, Blade went back to speak to the ambulance crew.

"When you get in there, be as careful as you can not to trample around or disturb anything." He showed his warrant card. "This is a crime scene."

"Right-oh, guv," said the driver, and she and her partner turned to drag their bulky bags from the cab. Blade studied the area carefully and stood in the doorway, watching them enter the building before following them.

He pointed to a trail of wet splotches that ran along the corridor from the entrance to Angela Liddell's open door. "Try to avoid those footprints."

Inside the room, he found Chaytor-Gill and Felicity Dumble, both in dressing gowns. His was silk in a paisley pattern. Blade recognised hers as the white one she had lent to Angela two days earlier. Angela was lying on the bed, half-covered by the crumpled bedclothes. There was blood on the sheets and pillowcase, and the angry red face he remembered from the interview was now ashen.

Adrian Harper was lying face down on the floor beside the bed. The male paramedic was already crouched beside him, while his partner was tending to Angela. Both were unconscious. Concerned, Blade bent down to look at his young constable. He straightened and turned to face the others.

"We haven't moved them," said the commandant. "We just checked that they were alive, then Mrs Dumble rang for the ambulance."

"Mmm . . ." Blade gestured towards the door. "Perhaps we should go out there while they're busy." Outside, he said, "Tell me what happened."

The pair looked at each other uncertainly for a moment. Chaytor-Gill began. "Well, we were woken at about two fifty by a loud scream." He went on hurriedly, "Er, we both arrived at our front doors at the same time. We have rooms opposite each other, down there . . ."

"Yes, yes, I know. Go on."

"We could hear noise coming from this direction but, well, it's damned cold out here and—"

"I suggested we put on our slippers and dressing gowns," added Felicity.

"Which we did," her boss resumed. "When we got here the noise had stopped. The door was open but the room was in darkness. We went in, put the light on, and . . . found this. Whoever did it had gone. Mrs Dumble used the phone in the room to call the ambulance while I checked their pulses."

"Mmm. You said noise. What sort of noise?"

"Well, apart from the initial screams which woke us up, it sounded like grunts and gasps, the sort people might make while fighting or wrestling. But I recognised the young man." The commandant looked at Blade accusingly. "I've seen him on your team. What on earth was an investigating officer doing in the room of a prime suspect in a murder case? Eh? Tell me that."

"Probably checking on her, as I ordered," Blade said mildly. "I asked your accommodation people to fix him up with a room." He pointed. "Probably that one. I passed it on the way in. The door's open and there's a light on."

"I knew nothing of that, why wasn't I informed?" Chaytor-Gill barked. "You've no right to approach my staff without asking me."

"You weren't here. You'd already left for London. Anyway, I wouldn't have thought you'd want to be troubled with such a trivial—"

"You could have asked my deputy," Chaytor-Gill blustered, cutting the detective short. "I need to be informed of everything that goes on here. I'd no idea this room was occupied. And on *my* corridor!"

"I'm sure the superintendent was simply trying to save us the bother," Felicity said soothingly.

Her boss failed to notice the apologetic shrug and sympathetic smile she directed to Blade. Not for the first time, he felt a warm glow in her presence. Even now, without make-up, in a dressing gown and slippers and her blonde hair tousled, she was stunning.

The door to Adrian's room was still ajar. Blade pushed it wide and they all stepped inside. There lay the coffee in a pool over the floor and the cup on its side. Nearer the door, the blanket made an untidy heap.

"Looks as though he made a quick exit," Felicity commented.

Blade nodded. "Yes. It ties in with what I was thinking. My guess is that, like you, he heard the screams and dashed straight in. Whoever it was must be a pretty tough nut because Harper's no pushover — he's built like a house. I'll get forensics in as soon as the ambulance people are done." He looked at them. "But you two must be tired. Thank you for what you did, but you should get back to your beds now. I may need to speak to you later in the day. I'm sorry I didn't consult you about the room, sir. I'll bear it in mind in future."

Chaytor-Gill acknowledged the apology with a stiff nod and turned away. His deputy smiled, surprising Blade with a conspiratorial wink.

He watched them walk back along the corridor. The warm feeling Felicity had aroused in him was mitigated by a sudden feeling of guilt. Was he responsible for the rift developing between him and Julie? Was the estrangement with his son his fault?

He went into Angela's room, where the paramedics had the casualties, both still unconscious, strapped to stretchers, ready to be wheeled to the ambulance.

"Anything you can tell me?" Blade asked.

The paramedic shrugged. "Not really. They both seem to have suffered severe blows to the head. The strange thing is that the woman has fresh cuts to her right wrist, which is probably where all the blood has come from. The doctors will be able to tell you more at the hospital after they've been assessed."

CHAPTER ELEVEN

THE ATMOSPHERE in the incident room was tense. Although it was not yet 7 a.m., they were all there, detectives and civilians alike. But there was none of the usual noisy banter. Instead, they congregated in small groups, whispering, asking each other what had brought them in so early.

John Hyde stood apart from the others, staring at the board and trying to avoid Dorothy's amused smile. She started to move across the room towards him. He swore under his breath. But it was futile trying to dodge her. After all, they had to work together.

"You'd better put the White Lady's picture up there," she said, nodding towards the board.

"Can't do that," he retorted. "She wouldn't show up in a photo." Then, abandoning his attempt at frivolity. "Anyway, as I said before, there's no such thing as ghosts. Ma'am."

Fortunately for Hyde, Dorothy's teasing was cut short by a civilian worker standing near enough to hear the exchange. "You're wrong there, Sergeant," he said, moving closer. "There's the White Lady, of course, but plenty of others too: fourteen, in fact."

They turned to see a short, round, rosy-cheeked man with a wide smile. His cherry-tomato nose and bushy eyebrows were topped by wispy strands of pale ginger hair that struggled unsuccessfully to cover an almost bald, freckled pate. He warmed to his theme.

"There's been books about them," he went on proudly in a broad Hampshire accent. "Bramshill's well-known as the most 'aunted 'ouse in 'Ampshire, and the ghosts are all well documented — all fourteen of 'em. Apart from the mistletoe-bough White Lady there's the Grey Lady, a Green Man and a young man dressed for tennis carrying a tennis racket. The ghost of a gardener has been seen near the lake . . . and visitors have *felt* the presence of a small girl when they were touched by her invisible hand. A man in a grey flannel suit has been seen to enter the hall through the open front door, and then walk straight through a solid wall on the other—"

The man was cut off in mid-flow by a loud clap. "Attention, please!" Blade called out, silencing the hushed voices.

After the ambulance had departed with Adrian Harper and Angela Liddell, Blade had returned to his office, where he went over the team's reports from the previous day and tried to make sense of the night's events. After using Adrian's bathroom to freshen up, he had just been provided with an early breakfast in the canteen.

"Thank you for braving the weather to get in at this unearthly hour, ladies and gentlemen," he began. "But it's going to be a busy day." He went on to relate the night's happenings, finishing with, "If you haven't had breakfast, it's laid on for you in the canteen. But I want all my team members to be next door and round the conference table at seven thirty."

* * *

Flanked by Dorothy and John Hyde, Blade gave the three other members of his team an update on what was known about the assaults on Angela Liddell and Adrian.

"First of all," he said, looking directly at PC Lucy Ramsey, "I've just heard that Adrian has recovered consciousness, which is good news, but he's badly concussed and can't remember anything about it. Lucy, I want you to go to the hospital and hold his hand. The moment he remembers anything — anything at all, no matter how small it is — I want to know immediately. You can also make regular checks on Miss Liddell. She's in a bad way but, hopefully, when she comes round, she might be able to give us a lead on her attacker."

Lucy's chair grated across the floor as she jumped up. Wincing, Blade gestured her to sit back down.

"Not yet. You can go as soon as this briefing is over. I want you to be fully up to date."

Looking disappointed, Lucy dragged her chair back to the table with another loud screech. Blade made a face.

"The commandant and his deputy were the first to arrive on the scene after hearing a scream from Liddell's room. They found her on the bed, unconscious. Adrian was lying on the floor, also out cold. They did what they could for them, rang for an ambulance, and then called me. Tony, as soon as we finish this meeting, I want you to take formal witness statements from both of them, separately. Don't let Mr Chaytor-Gill bully you into interviewing them together. Got it?"

Tony Robinson nodded. "Got it, sir."

"Good. I was next on the scene, arriving at the same time as the ambulance. While the crew were unloading their gear, I looked through the doorway into the accommodation block. There was a single track of wet footprints — on top of older, dried muddy ones —leading straight to Miss Liddell's room. I told the medics to try to avoid stepping on them in case forensics could get anything useful. Inside, Liddell and Adrian were in the positions as described by the commandant. The bedclothes were a bloody mess — literally, there was blood all over the place. The light was on when I arrived but it had been switched on by Mr Chaytor-Gill, who said that when he got there, the only illumination came from the corridor lamps."

Blade went on to relate the rest of his conversation with the commandant and his deputy and their visit to Adrian's room. The pair then departed to their own quarters. When the ambulance left with the casualties, he went back into Angela Liddell's room.

It was freezing in there — the window was wide open. This time, with all the stretchers and people out of the way, he could get across the room and look out at the lawn at the back of the building. The deep snow was untouched — except for a trail of footprints coming from the window. Careful not to disturb anything, he went out of the front entrance, walked round to the back and located the point where the footprints joined the road, where they disappeared, obliterated by car tyres and countless pairs of feet.

"Maybe forensics can get a print from the snow. We'll have to wait for their report, but they've promised a quick preliminary one," he added.

Blade then went on to detail the results of the visit he, Dorothy and John Hyde had made to London the previous day. He turned to DC Headley. "I read your report, Bill, including the results of your meeting with the security experts yesterday. Now, tell us your conclusions. I've said from the start that the CCTV camera facing the mistletoe-bough chest could tell us a lot. And?"

"It's really what the camera *can't* tell us that may help us most, sir," Headley said. "We've already established that the picture was frozen at certain times. Although this prevents us from seeing *what* happened, at least it tells us *when*. And yesterday we found out *how*. It's simple really. Apparently, every camera has a code number: feed that number into a mobile phone, point it at the camera, press the button and, bingo, the picture freezes until you click again to unlock it. All you need is the code number."

"So, who knows, or has access to, this number?" Hyde asked.

"The data is locked in a safe in the security office. Anyone on the staff would have access. Tony and I are still busy questioning them all and checking their records. Obviously, the manager, Mr Cotter, would have known it, but he's one of the murder victims, and we haven't been able to discover any link between him and Chief Superintendent Ashington. However, the pride Cotter took in his CCTV system was common knowledge. He might have boasted to somebody and let some vital detail slip. We're looking into that as well. It might lead us to the answer to the big question, which is, who?"

Blade stroked his chin thoughtfully. "I see where you're going, Bill. You think Cotter might have told someone — a person he could trust perhaps — how to disable a CCTV camera. Then, after Harold Ashington's death, Cotter might have put two and two together and come up with the identity of the killer. That could well be a motive for murdering him."

"That's what I was thinking, sir."

"Hmm . . . It's possible, Bill. Keep digging." Blade looked around at the others. "Anyone else have any ideas, or questions?"

Dorothy put her hand up. "Perhaps we're being too quick to presume Cotter's innocence. After all, he was the person best placed and able to deal with the camera."

"He wasn't even here," Hyde pointed out. "He was away, fishing."

"How do we know that for sure? It was all so vague. No one, not even his wife, knew where he was exactly." Dorothy paused, frowning. "Bill mentioned trying to find a link between Cotter and Ashington, who had a reputation for blackmail. Well, suppose he had something on Cotter."

"Like what?" Hyde said.

She shot him an exasperated look. "Consider this. What if Cotter and Angela Liddell were having an affair? Maybe he wasn't fishing at all but was holed up in her room. Ashington found out and was threatening to tell. We know there's already a connection between Liddell and Ashington, but maybe there's more to it than we thought. She could have lured him to her room. Then, a quick whisky-cyanide cocktail and job done. She's a strong lass. Between them, under cover of darkness, they could have smuggled the body into the mansion and dumped it in the chest. Cotter would easily have dealt with the camera."

"Mmm . . . but what about Cotter?" Blade said. "Why would she kill him? And why leave his body to be found in her own room?"

Dorothy shrugged. "Maybe she just doesn't like men. Maybe she's a use-'em-and-lose-'em type. And perhaps she thought that *we* would think she wouldn't be daft enough to kill a bloke in her own place. She came to us, remember, to report the body."

"Nice try, Dorothy, but I don't buy that one," said her boss. "Don't forget the cause of death was the same as Ashington's. Do you really think Cotter would have taken a whisky from her if he knew she was in the habit of lacing it with cyanide?"

She sighed. "Perhaps not. I was just trying to establish a link between them."

"And now she's in hospital, unconscious. I'm beginning to think that our Angela has been set up." Blade nodded to Lucy and smiled. "Off you go. Ring me when you get the latest on her and Adrian."

As Lucy left the conference room, Chaytor-Gill and Mrs Dumble came in.

"We've come to see if there's any news of your man and Miss Liddell," the commandant said.

"No news yet," Blade said. "PC Ramsay — you passed her in the doorway — is just on her way to the hospital to get the latest. I'll keep you informed. Thank you both for what you did last night."

"Least we could do." The commandant waved a hand. "I'm sure you'll find who is responsible for the attack. I have every confidence in you, Superintendent. You, er, have a good reputation at the Yard. I was there yesterday as it happens, and I was surprised to see your sergeant. Perhaps he told you? I was wondering . . . ?"

He was fishing. Blade decided to humour him. "Oh yes. I sent him there to inquire into Chief Superintendent Ashington's time at the Yard. I'd made an appointment for him to see an old colleague of mine, Superintendent Wriggley — we were together as young constables — but it turned out he was too busy, so he arranged for someone else to look after Sergeant Hyde."

Chaytor-Gill looked surprised. "Would that be *Jack* Wriggley?" He turned to Felicity. "We know him, don't we, Mrs Dumble."

"Yes, we do," she said. "He was here on a course at the beginning of the year, and he came back in the summer for our annual open day. Of course, he knew Harold Ashington from the Yard. His wife was here too. I remember seeing them all talking together—"

"Mrs Ashington? She was here?" Blade interrupted.

"That's right. There was a very good-looking young man with them, tall, fair-haired. I thought he must be the Ashingtons' son."

"*He* was here too?" Blade seemed to find this incredible.

"Yes, why not? It's a very popular family fun day out. My husband came," she glanced at the commandant, "and so did Mrs Chaytor-Gill." She looked at her watch. "I must run. I'm due to give a lecture in five minutes."

Before she could escape, Blade said quickly, "I wonder if, after your lecture, you'd be kind enough to come back and give DC Robinson over there your formal witness statement about last night." He indicated to Tony, still seated at the table. He turned back to the commandant. "And if you, sir, would like to give yours now, while you're here?"

"I could come back later with Mrs D. Two birds with one stone and all that—"

Blade held up his hand. "I'm sorry, sir, but the statements must be independent."

"Of course." Chaytor-Gill smiled. "Silly of me. I should have known better. No collusion, eh? Now will be fine."

CHAPTER TWELVE

"WELL, THERE'S a surprise," said Blade. He, Dorothy and Hyde were gathered in his office. "I think we're going to have to take another, closer look at Sylvia Ashington. If all her candid garrulity was meant to put us off the scent, it was pretty effective. What was it she said? 'My boyfriend, Jack', 'right under his nose' and 'he never guessed'."

"Am I missing something?" Hyde asked.

"When we interviewed her, Sylvia told us that she had a lover called Jack," Dorothy said.

"And if that Jack turns out to be Wriggley of the Yard, it would account for her 'right under his nose' remark," Blade continued. "It could also be another reason to fob you off with a sergeant, John, to avoid having anything to do with your investigation. If his involvement with Sylvia were to come out, it would almost certainly scupper his chances for promotion — and provide a possible motive for murder. Anyway, we can have another go at Sylvia this afternoon. I've arranged for her to come in to make her statement."

"But she has a solid alibi," Hyde pointed out. "She'd been to see her doctor and wouldn't have had time to get here."

"She didn't need to be here if she didn't actually do the deed, but she could have been complicit. Wriggley could have called on Ashington and given him the whisky. She could have joined her boyfriend later to help him to dump the body in the chest," Blade said.

"Why bother to move him? Presumably, Ashington would have taken the fatal dose in his room. Why not just leave the body there, out of sight? It wouldn't have been discovered until somebody realised Ashington was missing when he failed to turn up for lectures. Surely they wouldn't take the huge risk of humping a body around the campus?" said Hyde.

"I don't know," Blade said, wearily. "Maybe not. I can't think straight. I've been here since three o'clock this morning. Let's wait and see what Sylvia has to say for herself."

"And then there's the other piece of information Mrs Dumble gave us," Dorothy said, staring directly into her chief's eyes. "She saw all three of them — Sylvia, Jack and Ashington — together at the college's open day. And they had a young man with them who she thought might be the Ashingtons' son. And from her brief description . . ."

She paused — the implication was left hanging in the air with her stare still unwavering. "Sir, I really do think it's time I interviewed your son Richard."

Blade closed his eyes for a moment. "I'll give you his number. Make an appointment to see him in Loughborough tomorrow and get back as soon as you can. Drive up, it'll be quicker. While you're there, I'll go up to the Yard to see Jack the lad. I'll surprise him, so he won't have time to think of an excuse to dodge me. But that's for tomorrow. This afternoon we can see what Sylvia's got to say for herself. I want you both back here at two o'clock."

* * *

Lucy Ramsey was back at Bramshill shortly before midday. She found Blade in the incident room with Dorothy, huddled at a desk, heads close, peering at a computer screen.

Hearing her approach, her boss looked up at her. "Ah! The very person. We were just wondering how you were doing. Let's hear your news. Find a seat and join us."

Lucy fetched a chair and sat down. She told them that the medical staff had still been busy with Angela Liddell when she arrived at the hospital, so she had spent more than an hour with Adrian who, despite still having a very sore head, was delighted to see her. She blushed slightly.

"They say he'll be okay, but they want to keep him in for a day or two." She pulled a notebook from her bag and read from her notes. "He's badly concussed from a heavy blow to the back of the head, and he says it hurts to think, but he now remembers hearing Inspector Liddell screaming. He ran into her room, which was dimly lit, and saw Angela on the bed, a man kneeling over her. She was struggling to fight him off and doing pretty well. The man had his back to him, so he couldn't see his face. He thinks he was wearing an anorak with the hood up. Adrian recalls diving onto the bed and grappling with him . . . and then nothing, until he woke up in hospital this morning."

Leaving out the bit where she had taken Blade's instructions literally and held Adrian's hand, Lucy continued. "I did get to see Miss Liddell eventually, but she's still unconscious. She's on a drip and is wired up to various machines. The consultant is hopeful that she'll pull through all right, but we'll have to wait until she comes around before we see if there's any brain damage. It was a particularly severe blow, much harder than the one that knocked out Adrian. 'Savage', the doctor called it. He thought she could have been struck by a heavy club or truncheon. But here's the odd thing. There was a laceration on the inside of Miss Liddell's right wrist, as though she'd slashed it herself. The cut was deep and it must have bled profusely."

"Yes, the paramedics did mention the cut wrist," Blade said. "It does seem odd." He turned his attention back to the computer screen. "Forensics have sent their report and we were just looking at it when you arrived. It says here . . . Now where was it? Here it is. 'Fresh blood found on nail scissors found on the floor beside the bed matches that of Angela Liddell, tested previously. Partial fingerprints on the scissors also match Miss Liddell's.'"

"She couldn't possibly have been in the act of committing suicide just as the attacker struck," Dorothy said. "That's beyond belief."

Blade stroked his chin — another habit of his, less irritating than the clapping. "No. But what if the intruder's aim was to fake her suicide, and he hadn't intended to hit her. If you remember, I suggested earlier that Angela might have been set up — the poisoned whisky conveniently left in her room, for instance. If she were then to be found dead with her wrists cut, we might be expected to think she'd decided she couldn't get away with murder and the only way out was to take her own life." He was silent for a few moments. "But suppose the attacker got into her room and managed to slash just one wrist as she slept . . . and then it all went pear-shaped when she woke up and screamed, so he panicked and hit her. She wasn't meant to wake up because," Blade leaned forward and read from the forensics report, "'a three-quarters-full cup of milk laced with a strong sedative was found on the bedside table.' Possibly she only drank a little, maybe it tasted odd. Anyway, she woke up and made a noise. Then Adrian arrived, and the attacker knocked him out. Thinking he'd silenced Angela for good, the attacker escaped through the window."

Dorothy wasn't convinced. "That would mean someone would have visited Angela to give her the milk. Adrian would have noticed them going into her room."

"Perhaps he did. We don't know yet. He might not remember. He could have missed a visitor — after all, he couldn't watch the corridor all night."

Lucy jumped to Adrian's defence. "As you say, he couldn't watch the corridor all night. What I don't understand is how he was overcome so quickly. He was tackling a man who was kneeling on the bed and whose back was toward him. So, how come Adrian was hit on the back of his head? How did the attacker manage to do that when he was facing away and already struggling with Miss Liddell?"

Blade nodded. "Good question, Lucy. When I arrived on the scene, Adrian was lying on the floor beside the bed, as though he had fallen forwards and slightly to the left. Which made me wonder . . ."

". . . If there were *two* intruders," Dorothy finished his thought.

* * *

Sylvia chatted away as breezily as when Blade and Dorothy had visited her at home. Still elegant, immaculately groomed and expensively dressed, although the tweed outfit was different and had the addition of a warm, padded coat with sturdy sheepskin-lined boots.

She halted in the doorway to Blade's office and surveyed the superintendent, flanked by Dorothy and John Hyde. She gave them a broad grin. "'Ello, 'ello, 'ello. What's all this then, the bloody Spanish Inquisition? I've only come to give my statement."

"Sergeant Hyde will take your statement," Blade said without a flicker of a smile. "You are under caution, and you will be asked to sign it. Please take a seat."

She glanced back at the civilian who had shown her in. "Ooh, doesn't he sound serious?" She shrugged off her coat. "Can you take this, dear, and hang it up somewhere? It's warm in here."

The civilian departed, closing the door behind her. Sylvia sat on the vacant chair on the other side of the table, facing the three detectives. Hyde switched on the recorder, announced who was present and stated that the interview with Mrs Sylvia Ashington was starting at 2.21 p.m.

Sylvia's smile was replaced by a frown. "What *is* this? And what did you mean by 'under caution?' That's for suspects, isn't it?"

Blade merely pursed his lips.

"You know damn well that I couldn't have killed Harold." Sylvia shouted. "You told me yourself what the time of his death was, and you knew I couldn't have been at Bramshill then. I was in my doctor's surgery, and I know you checked that."

"That's right," Blade said. "But you could have colluded with the killer. It's called aiding and abetting and is a punishable crime."

"That's rubbish, and you know it."

"You know the layout at Bramshill, you've been there before. I know you were at the open day, and you went into your husband's room. Did another visitor accompany you?"

"So. What if he did?"

"*So*, your accomplice — who obviously knew Ashington — could have called on him the day of the murder. After the killing, he could have lain low in the room until you arrived in the evening to help him move the body. Who was the other man, Sylvia?"

"Oh, give me strength!" But she looked wary.

"Could it be your boyfriend, Jack, the one you told us about the other day? Right under Harold's nose and he never suspected, you said." Blade paused. "Guess where Sergeant Hyde was when we were speaking to you. I'll tell you. He was at Scotland Yard talking to Superintendent Wriggley. *Jack* Wriggley, whose office is less than a stone's throw from what used to be Harold Ashington's. Under his nose."

"What if it was near Harold's?" She looked truly worried now. "You're trying to set me up."

"Did Superintendent Wriggley go with you to the open day, Sylvia? Or did he 'just happen' to meet you there? You were seen talking together — you, Jack and Harold. We have witnesses."

"Yes," Sylvia snarled viciously. "And I'll tell you who else was there with my husband. Your bloody son, Richard."

* * *

It was four thirty before Sylvia left for home, her written statement completed and signed. Blade called a final, short meeting to brief Lucy, Headley and Robinson about their duties for the following day.

"John, Inspector Fraser will be away, so you'll be in charge here until I get back from London, probably in the afternoon. But I think we can all go home now. We've all had an early start."

Outside, he slumped wearily into the driving seat of his car and knuckled his bloodshot eyes. He had been on the go since three a.m. and the day stretched endlessly behind him. Was it really only today that he'd seen PC Harper and a bloodied Angela Liddell lying in her room unconscious? And then there were Dorothy's words. They rang in his brain.

Unless there were two.

And Sylvia Ashington screaming at him.

Your bloody son, Richard.

No. That was silly. He couldn't seriously make that connection. And yet . . . He thought back to the time, just a few days ago, when he'd seen Harold Ashington's body in the chest. Afterwards, he'd sat in the car outside the mansion and groaned aloud.

What have you bloody done, Julie?

Silly? Maybe. But the fact was, he had suspected Julie. She had lied to him about where she was that night. And Richard? Had he lied too? Were they in it together somehow?

He lowered his head into his hands, ashamed of even imagining such perfidy. This was his wife, for heaven's sake, his son. It was Dorothy's suggestion that there might have been *two* killers that had triggered these flights of treacherous fancy.

But her idea did have some merit. There could be two killers. He smiled grimly. Tomorrow he would interview his old colleague, Jack Wriggley, the supposed lover of the murdered man's widow.

Blade started the car and drove off, his tired mind still in turmoil.

* * *

Dorothy stepped in out of the cold and shut the door behind her. She jogged on the spot to dislodge the snow from her shoes and kicked them off. She sniffed. The tantalising aroma intensified as the door to the kitchen opened and Bob greeted her with a kiss and a hug.

"Hi, you're early. I've been slaving over a hot stove. Roast spuds, green beans, carrots," he assumed a bad French accent, "but you vill 'ave to wait while I give zer finishing touch to zer fillet steak."

He blew a kiss.

Laughing, she peeped into the kitchen. The table had been set with a clean cloth, the best cutlery, napkins, glasses and a candle waiting to be lit. A bottle of red wine had already been opened.

"I thought it would be cosier in here," Bob said. "It's a bit chilly in the dining room."

"Perfect. Who's a clever boy then? While you're doing the steak, I'll pop up for a quick bath and get changed."

She gave him another kiss and ran up the stairs.

"I certainly picked a good mother-in-law," she commented later, popping a grape into her mouth. "That was a lovely meal. Your mum trained you very well."

He grinned. "And now you're training me to do *your* job. I'm sorry there was no pudding, by the way. I didn't have time. I was too busy working for you."

She leaned forward, serious now. "So, how did you get on?"

"Well, you're right as usual, Clever Clogs. The post of Chief Inspector of Constabulary is shortly to become vacant — and guess who's the hot favourite? Yep, your man, Mr Roderick Chaytor-Gill."

"I knew it!"

"He might not get it of course. There are other strong candidates. But that's not all. There are four Inspectors of Constabulary — and apparently one of those is also due for retirement, so there'll be another top job up for grabs. Your Roddy could get that if he misses out as chief." Bob's brow wrinkled in puzzlement. "I don't understand your interest in this. Surely, you don't think—?"

"Of course not," Dorothy cut in quickly with a laugh. "No motive. And he wasn't even there for the second murder. I just like to get the *feel* of things, that's all. It's a strange atmosphere there — a world-famous police college is closing, and no one seems to give a damn. Not a word of protest. Maybe that's because the top dogs will be taken care of, most of the instructors are serving police officers — chief inspectors and above — and they'll simply go back to their own stations."

"There must be a lot of civilian workers though," Bob said.

"Yeah, their jobs will go. I know it's expensive and money must be saved. It's these blasted cuts," she added bitterly. "Perhaps Bramshill's a different case, but the training centres for new recruits have gone too, and it seems to me that the future for the police service is bleak to say the—"

Rolling his eyes, Bob pretended to play a violin, caught her warning look and hastily changed the subject. "So, how was your day?"

"Don't ask!" she said, telling him anyway. "It started with one of our constables and one of our prime suspects in hospital. This is all off the record, by the way."

He nodded. "Of course."

She went on to recount the events of the day. This was how they'd always worked together, from the days when he was a reporter on the *Shields Gazette* and she was climbing the ladder from detective constable to sergeant and now, inspector. As an outsider, he sometimes noticed details she'd missed and made useful suggestions. Often, he would use his own contacts to ferret out information that would help her investigations. When a case was over and he could write about it, his inside knowledge gave him a better, more accurate story. He always made sure never to use information that might compromise Dorothy's relationship with her colleagues or superiors. She trusted him implicitly.

"So, tomorrow," she concluded, "I'm off to Loughborough to see Richard. The boss isn't too happy about it, but he knows it has to be done. He brightened up a bit at my suggestion that there might be two villains, so he's going to question his old chum Wriggley, who, along with Sylvia, *does* have a motive for murder."

"For Ashington's murder, maybe," Bob said doubtfully. "But why would he hang around to move the body? He could have just left him in his quarters. And what motive could there be to kill the security chap and then to attack your copper and Angela Liddell?"

"I know," Dorothy said, "that's been worrying me too. Perhaps the two killings aren't connected at all, and there are indeed two murderers, but working independently." She sighed and shook her head. "Oh, I dunno. Come on, let's have an early night while we have the chance. I'll give you a hand to load the dishwasher."

* * *

John Hyde was in buoyant mood when he parked outside his cottage in Odiham. Becky was busy in the kitchen. He lifted her off her feet, swung her around and kissed her.

"Ah, that smells good. What have we got?"

"Roast chicken with all the trimmings, roast potatoes, carrots, broccoli and parsnips."

"And bread sauce?" he said hopefully.

"Oh, I never thought, but I'll make some if you like." She paused. "It's not actually a *whole* chicken, but I've added some streaky bacon. It only takes fifty minutes to cook."

"Sounds great. Never mind the bread sauce, it'll be quicker without."

"You seem chipper tonight," Becky said. "I was expecting you to be feeling down after a day of being teased about ghosts by Dorothy."

"Oh, that," he said dismissively. "She didn't say much, although one of the civvies gave me a lecture about the ghosts of Bramshill. The place seems to be overrun with them."

He went on to tell her about the attacks on Adrian and Angela, "for your ears only. But the reason for me being so chipper is because I," he tapped his chest importantly, "am going to be in charge tomorrow. The boss and Dorothy are both going to be away. Those constables will wish they'd never been born. I'll run them ragged." He grinned evilly.

She laughed. "That'll be the day. I'll bet they know more about the job than you do. Well, I've got some news as well. Open a bottle of wine while I dish up. I'll tell you about it while we eat."

When they were seated at the table, he shot her a slightly worried look and asked, "Well, what's your news then?"

"What do you think?"

"I don't know," he said apprehensively. "You tell me."

"I've got a job! I went for the interview this morning, and this afternoon they rang to say I'd got it. It's at the hairdressers in Hartley Wintney, near where your boss lives. It's just a short bus ride from here, via Hook, and I start next week."

"Wow! That's wonderful." He smiled in relief and raised his glass. "Cheers!"

* * *

There were no celebrations in the Blade household. He too found his wife in the kitchen, but his welcome was almost as chilly as the weather outside.

"You're early." Julie sounded more accusing than pleased. "You should have rung. I haven't even started the dinner yet. Go and read the paper or something while I see what I can cobble together."

"I'm sorry. I thought . . ." his words trailed away. She had her back to him, the fridge door open, and was studying the contents.

Blade hesitated, shrugged and headed upstairs. As he showered and changed into more comfortable clothes, his puzzlement began to give way to resentment. Why was Julie being so hostile? For goodness sake, he'd been up since three that morning. Couldn't she be a bit more sympathetic?

She soon called up to him that the meal was on the table. As she dished up, he felt impelled to break the uneasy silence that prevailed.

"That was quick," he said, forcing a note of brightness into his tone. "Very nice too," he added, forking up some of the stir fry she had prepared out of the leftovers from a previous meal — roast lamb and a selection of vegetables.

When Julie remained silent, he forged ahead. "Funny how something you 'cobble up' in a hurry turns out to be really tasty."

"What's that supposed to mean?" she snapped. "That my proper meals are rubbish?"

"Of course not. I simply meant . . ." His cheery tone gave way to one of exasperation. "For pity's sake, Julie, what the hell's the matter with you? I've had an absolutely bloody awful day, then I come home to find you like a wet weekend."

She glared at him. "I've been speaking to Richard. He tells me you're sending Dorothy to see him tomorrow."

"I'm not sending her. She wants to go. I told you she wants to speak to him to set her own mind at rest—"

"Well tell her she can't and set *my* mind at rest. You're the boss, aren't you?"

"You know that everyone connected with this affair, however slightly, has to be questioned. If it isn't done properly, I'll be taken off the case, and then I won't be in a position to help anyone, never mind Richard." His eyes narrowed. "Did you know that he went to Bramshill's open day with Ashington?"

She set her fork down. "No, I didn't."

"Well, he did. The commandant and his deputy saw him. They thought he must be Ashington's son. So you see, the boy hasn't told us everything. That's what prompted Dorothy to go to Loughborough tomorrow. I'm going up to London to inter-view another suspect." He looked closely at her. "We're testing a new theory, that there might be *two* killers working together."

When she didn't react, he pushed his chair back. "I'm going to bed. I'm dog tired."

"Yes, you must be. But you haven't finished your dinner."

"I'm not hungry now. I just need sleep. And so do you. When I left at three this morning, you were freezing cold. You'd been up and were only just coming to bed."

Julie nodded. "Yes, I stayed downstairs to have a cup of tea and catch up on some TV programmes I'd recorded, but I had a lie-in until after nine. By the way, what was the emergency?"

He told her about the attacks on Adrian and Angela and went upstairs, recalling how cold Julie had been when she had got into bed. Had she really been watching TV? Had she been outside? The questions continued to chase each other around in his mind until, eventually, he dropped off. He fell asleep with the comforting thought that Angela had screamed at 2.50 a.m. and Julie was in bed by three.

Julie must surely be in the clear. She couldn't possibly have driven the eight miles home from Bramshill in ten minutes.

CHAPTER THIRTEEN

JOHN HYDE arrived in the incident room at nine fifteen the following morning to find Bill Headley and Tony Robinson crouched in front of a computer.

Bill looked up. "Morning, Sarge," he said, poking the cuff of his shirt back to stare ostentatiously at his watch.

The sergeant grinned. "Very funny, Bill. I had to pick the boss up on my way in and run him to the station. I might give one of you the job of fetching him back this afternoon." He nodded towards the computer. "Anything interesting?"

"It's the full forensic report on yesterday's crime scene," Tony said. "The attack on Adrian and Inspector Liddell. I'll print it for you."

"I'll be in the boss's office. Bring it in and we'll have a . . . a mini-conference." He looked around. Where's Lucy?"

"Up at the hospital, getting the latest on the casualties," Bill said, and winked. "I think she wanted an excuse to see Adrian."

Later, when the three of them were seated around Blade's desk, Hyde read quickly through the printout.

"This doesn't take us any further than yesterday's preliminary report," he said. "We'll leave it here for the boss to see." A shadow darkened the doorway. "Can I help you, sir?" Hyde asked.

"I'm looking for Superintendent Blade," the commandant said.

"He's out, sir. He'll be back late this afternoon. Is there anything I can do for you?"

Chaytor-Gill hesitated. "No, not really. I happened to mention some people who came to our open day and . . . no, no, it doesn't matter."

Before the visitor could leave, Hyde said quickly, "The superintendent briefed us about them, sir, so if there's anything else you can add that might help us . . . ?"

"Well, it's just a picture." The commandant hesitated, then held out a large envelope. "The official photographer took it. It shows me talking to a group that includes all the people I spoke about. I've captioned it."

Hyde took the envelope. "Thank you very much, sir. That's great. I'll make sure he sees it as soon as he gets back."

He waited until the commandant had gone before slitting open the envelope. Then, as another figure darkened the doorway, he laid it flat on the desk. "Well, look what the wind's blown in!"

Lucy walked in, smiling, followed by a sheepish-looking Adrian Harper, wearing a large bandage around his head. The three detectives gathered around him, pumping his hand and congratulating him on his speedy recovery. While Lucy was despatched to fetch him a cup of coffee, he admitted that he still had a slight headache and was a bit wobbly on his feet, but he was anxious not to miss out on the investigation.

Lucy returned with a tray of coffees for them all, so they moved from Blade's small office and sat down at one end of the large conference table in the outer room. Hyde took the commandant's envelope with him.

"Well, the very latest is this," he told Adrian, drawing out the picture, while they crowded around to look. The photograph showed a casually dressed group of eight people, all smiling happily. A neatly printed caption, taped to the bottom, read: *Left to right: Mr Roderick Chaytor-Gill, Mrs Felicity Dumble, Mr Richard (Ashington?), Mr Harold Ashington, Mr Keith Dumble, Mrs Anthea Chaytor-Gill, Supt. Jack Wriggley and Mrs Sylvia Ashington.*

"I didn't know our murder victim had a son," Lucy said, tapping Richard's image.

"He didn't," Hyde said shortly, suddenly aware that he was the only one present who knew Richard's true identity. And he had been sworn to silence.

"Perhaps we'd better trace him then," Lucy persisted. She grinned at Adrian. "That could be a job for me. I wouldn't mind interviewing him, he's very good looking, isn't he?"

"They're quite a handsome bunch altogether," Bill Healey observed.

"Yeah," Tony Robinson agreed. "The commandant's missus is a dish."

They all stared at the image of Anthea Chaytor-Gill. Shorter than the others, her slender figure was set off to perfection by a flowery summer dress. She had a wide, generous mouth and a flawless complexion. Her beautifully cut hair was almost as black as her husband's.

"Mmm . . . very nice," Bill conceded, studying her legs, "but I still think Mrs Dumble has more style. Now she has a classy elegance that—"

"Okay, folks." Hyde, anxious to shift attention away from Richard, hastily snatched up the picture. "The Miss World contest is over. Let's get down to some real work. Are you two still tied up with the CCTV business?"

"No, Sarge," Bill replied. "We've gone as far as we can for the moment."

Hyde stroked his chin, unconsciously emulating his boss. He had the photograph in his hand and was staring at it, thinking hard. Blade had left him in charge for the day and would expect him to use his initiative and do some good work. And he was anxious to please. He clapped his hands, another of his boss's irritating habits.

"Right. Let's get down to business. Remember Inspector Fraser's suggestion at yesterday's conference that there might be a *pair* of killers?" Bill, Tony and Lucy nodded in unison. "Well, Superintendent Blade was quite taken with the idea, which is why he's not here today. He's gone to interview Superintendent Wriggley who, apparently, has been having it off with Sylvia Ashington."

The sergeant put the picture back down on the table. "Have you noticed anything else about this photo?" He looked at each of them in turn. When no one answered, he said, "There's another couple in it who know Bramshill well, they're often here — Mr Keith Dumble and Mrs Anthea Chaytor-Gill."

His companions wriggled uncomfortably in their chairs, unhappy about where this was heading. They said nothing.

"Bill, I want you and Tony to see what you can find out about Mr Dumble, and, Lucy, you can do the same regarding Mrs Chaytor-Gill. Don't speak to either of them. Just nose around their home patches, chat to the neighbours perhaps, see if you can pick up any gossip. You can get the commandant and his deputy's home addresses from Admin. No need to mention names, just say you want to look at the staff lists."

"Are you sure that we . . . ?" Bill began hesitantly.

"We have to investigate everything thoroughly," Hyde insisted. "Just get on with it."

"Shall I go with Lucy?" Adrian asked.

"Absolutely not. That knock on the head must have scattered any brains you might have had to begin with. You shouldn't even be here, you're on the sick list."

"I'm okay. I've had worse injuries than this playing rugby and still carried on working."

"Have you been signed off by the doctor? Have you got a note?"

"No."

"That settles it. Get off home."

"He could come with me for the ride, to keep me company," Lucy said. "He wouldn't be doing any work, or even have to drive if we took my car."

Hyde sighed. "So long as I don't know about it." He turned to face Adrian. "Just don't forget, I've told you, officially, to go home."

* * *

Blade bought a first class ticket, settled into a quiet seat and placed an open notebook on the table in front of him, jotting down occasional thoughts and possible answers to the many questions that crowded his mind.

Why had Julie showed no surprise or curiosity when he said there might be *two* killers? Was that because she knew already? Could she really be in collusion with — he suddenly felt sick at the idea — Richard? He remembered his suspicions as he'd driven home the night before.

Had they planned the killing some time ago? Maybe Richard had mentioned meeting Ashington in Loughborough, and she had felt she needed to tell him about their relationship. Could she have gone on to voice her fears that he, Blade, might take some action that could jeopardise his own career if he learned that Ashington was back in their lives? Was that the moment the seed of murder had been planted in her mind in the mistaken belief that she would be protecting her husband? His stomach lurched.

He remembered her words when he'd confronted her after seeing Ashington's body: *I thought you'd find him and do something silly. I thought you'd kill him.*

He remembered her lie about a late night walk on the common — a clumsy attempt to hide the fact that she'd gone to the King's Head to meet Harold Ashington. Richard had been in the pub at the same time, although she'd denied seeing him. Richard had admitted to seeing his mother but said he'd kept out of sight. Was he lying as well?

No, that didn't make sense, because at that time Ashington was already dead. He had been murdered early that afternoon.

Had Richard arrived much earlier than he said — after lunch time, perhaps — visited Ashington in his room and poisoned him? With cyanide? How and where on earth would he or Julie have got that?

Did they go back to Bramshill that night to move the body? If so, why? Just to confuse the police? No, too risky, surely. Would Richard have known how to freeze the CCTV screen? Possibly. He had grown up with the new technology. But how could he have obtained the code number to dial?

Afterwards, had they returned to Richard's room at the King's Head to correlate their stories in case they were questioned? They couldn't go home because they wouldn't want Blade to know that Richard was in the area.

The detective wrestled with the questions but was no nearer to finding answers when the train drew into Paddington. As he put his things away, he took comfort from his earlier conclusion that Julie could not have attacked Angela Liddell at 2.50 a.m. and be home in bed ten minutes later.

He wondered uneasily how Dorothy would fare with Richard.

* * *

Dorothy's journey to Loughborough was surprisingly easy. No fresh snow had fallen since the M4 and M1 had been cleared and gritted overnight, but a bleak forecast had kept many drivers off the roads and traffic was light.

She had chosen to meet Richard at the Burleigh Court hotel because it was conveniently situated on the university campus. She pulled into the car park almost forty minutes early for the 11 a.m. appointment, giving her plenty of time to freshen up, find a quiet corner in the lounge and arrange two armchairs facing each other, with a low table in between.

Richard arrived exactly on time. He hesitated at the doorway, his gaze roaming over the half dozen or so people in the room. She stood up and waved, recognising him at once from a photograph she'd seen in the Blades' sitting room. He threaded his way towards her between the armchairs.

"I'm Detective Inspector Dorothy Fraser. You're very punctual. It's good of you to come." Smiling, she shook his hand and, to put him at his ease, added, "My word, Richard, aren't you like your mum!"

"So they say." There was no answering smile. "It's only a few hundred yards and I came on my bike. I had to leave halfway through a lecture."

"I'm sorry about that, but there are a few things we need to clear up." She paused as a waiter approached with a laden tray. "Ah, here's the coffee and biscuits." She pointed towards a chair. "I've ordered sandwiches at lunchtime and we could have a bowl of soup too, if you like — to warm us up in this cold weather. Your dad's paying!"

"Lunch?" he said, sounding taken aback. "How long is this going to take? I've already told my father all I know. I've got lectures this afternoon as well as other work to catch up on."

Dorothy sat down facing him. She had positioned the chairs carefully to give herself a view of the lounge, while all Richard could see was part of the blank wall behind her head. This made it difficult for him to avoid the piercing gaze she now directed at him. Already she was beginning to dislike her boss's son. Her smile had gone, and she spoke sharply.

"I shan't keep you any longer than necessary, but your work didn't stop you trotting off all day when Mr Ashington called you, did it? And that wasn't the only time you neglected your studies. You were at Bramshill for the open day, weren't you — again not bothering to tell your parents — so you must be familiar with the layout of the college including, no doubt, Mr Ashington's living quarters."

"I explained all that. Mr Ashington wanted to keep it a secret. It was all supposed to be a surprise for Dad—"

"It was that all right." Dorothy gave a short, humourless laugh and picked up her notebook from the table. "Your father asked you to try to think of anyone who might recall seeing you in London at around one or two o'clock. So, have you?"

"No. I didn't talk to anyone. Like I told him, I just wandered around. I bought some sandwiches, but I can't remember the name of the shop or where it is. There was a queue and I don't think I even spoke to the girl at the checkout. I just paid and left, so there was no reason for her to have noticed me in particular — unless, of course, she was bowled over by my good looks."

His half-hearted attempt at humour fell flat.

"You do realise that we're trying to verify your alibi and prove you really were where you say you were at the time of the murder? Did you book a ticket for the ten fifteen train in advance?"

He shook his head. "I bought it at the ticket office."

"Did you pay by credit or debit card?"

"Cash. Mr Ashington was going to repay me."

"So, there's nothing to prove you caught that train. You see, Richard, for all we know, you might have travelled earlier and have had much more time to get to Bramshill." Dorothy thought for a moment. "They're bound to have cameras at Loughborough station. I'll have a look to see if you can be spotted boarding that train, and we can check at the other end too. You might have been pictured leaving the train at Euston."

He shifted uncomfortably, silent under her stony stare until, finally, Dorothy leaned back in her chair. Her expression softened.

"You're working hard, then, nose to the grindstone. Chemistry, isn't it?" She spoke kindly.

Richard nodded, obviously relieved at the change of subject.

"That must be really difficult," Dorothy said. "I dropped all the sciences at school. I hated the smells in the chemistry laboratory, but the other girls didn't seem to mind." The childhood memory seemed to bring her Geordie accent to the fore. "I suppose you'll do a lot of lab work as part of your course?"

His face brightened. "That's the best part."

"And can you mess about doing your own thing like? Experiments?"

"Sometimes, yes."

"Ee, fancy!" Dorothy leaned forward. Suddenly her expression hardened, and her voice became harsh again. The accent disappeared.

"*You'll have the opportunity and the know-how to make cyanide, then.*"

* * *

"This is a nice surprise," said Superintendent Wriggley, coming around his desk to greet Blade. "You should have let me know you were coming."

So you could have invented an excuse to be away, his visitor thought. It was to avoid that possibility that he had persuaded the receptionist to show him up to Wriggley's office unannounced, so that he could surprise his 'old friend.'

"After all those years, eh, where have they flown? Is this just a social call, Ralph, or an official one to do with Ashington's death? Poor old Harold, eh? Although, as I recall, you had no reason to like the man."

"Neither did you, Jack."

"Ha!" Wriggley barked. His welcoming smile turned bleak. "Yes, he did lead the pair of us a merry dance when he was our sergeant, didn't he? But after you left, I never gave him the chance to fault me." He gave a satisfied smirk. "I was never more than one or two steps behind him."

"And now," Blade said mildly, "you've caught up with him. Word has it that you are in line for his job. Chief Super no less. Poor old Ashington indeed. And I'll bet it won't be long before you make commander, the rank the late but unlamented Harold was aiming for."

Wriggley went back behind his desk and sat down. "Come off it, Ralph. You can't really believe I bumped the bugger off just to get his job. That's hardly a motive for murder."

110

Uninvited, Blade settled in a chair facing his former colleague across the desk. His lips were pursed. "Mmm, maybe not, but if you include his wife — Sylvia refers to you as 'my Jack,' by the way — not to mention her very valuable house, they all add up to a pretty strong motive."

Wriggley was on his feet again, his face red. "Are you accusing me of something? Arresting me? Charging me?"

"No, of course not. I have no proof of anything — yet."

"Then get out of here. I can make things very awkward for you if I decide to tell your chiefs about your wife's previous relationship with Ashington."

"They already know."

Wriggley blinked. "Then things could be very awkward for them too. You shouldn't be on this case at all. If I report—"

Blade's contemptuous laugh cut him short. "Seems we've both learned the art of craftiness from Harold Ashington. See what I mean? You threaten me and, tit for tat, I threaten you. So, consider this, Jack. If your relationship with the lovely Sylvia were to come to light, your own career would come off the rails big time."

Wriggley leaned forward, snatched up the phone and pressed a key. "Would you send someone to show my visitor out."

The two superintendents stood glaring at each other until a uniformed constable arrived to escort Blade from the building.

The receptionist looked up and smiled as Blade passed her desk. "Was he surprised?"

"Very."

* * *

"Excuse me. Are you all right?" She pointed at Adrian, sitting beside Lucy. "Is he ill? You've been sitting on my wall for over ten minutes. I've been watching you from my lounge window."

The speaker was a diminutive woman of about fifty, slightly built with elegantly styled blonde hair, smooth skin and even features. But her looks were marred by expression-less grey eyes and thin, cruel lips.

The garden path had been cleared of snow, so the woman still wore fur-lined slippers. Apart from this incon-gruous note, she was tastefully dressed in a deep red woollen jacket and skirt over a high-necked cashmere jumper. What little jewellery she had looked expensive.

She looked, Adrian Harper thought, like a lady who lunched — and possibly gossiped.

"I'm perfectly okay, ma'am, thank you." He stood up, unfurling himself to his full height.

She leaned backwards slightly to look up at him and stared at the bandage on his head. "Oh. I thought perhaps you were ill when I saw . . ."

He grinned and patted the dressing. "No, no, I'm fine. This is just—"

"Then what are you both doing sitting on my wall, loi-tering?" Her voice was clipped, commanding. She was not at all intimidated by Adrian's bulk.

Lucy stood up and fished around in her shoulder bag to retrieve her warrant card.

"We're not loitering, madam," she said. "We're police officers. I am Constable Lucy Ramsay, and this is Constable Harper."

Adrian produced his own card. "We're making inquiries in the area as part of an investigation."

The woman studied both cards carefully, comparing their faces to the photographs on their cards.

"Well," she said with some asperity, "I can't imagine what you might find to investigate around here. This is a short cul-de-sac, as you can see, and I assure you it's *very* respectable."

"I can see that." Adrian looked around him.

There were just thirteen 1930s-built detached red-brick houses, six on each side and another straddling the end of the short road. Each had been built in a different style and they all stood in large gardens that, in summer, would be shaded by the various well-established trees that now stretched their bare arms across the lawns and flower beds that slept under their blanket of snow.

Adrian wondered idly if he would ever be able to afford to live in such a place. Unlikely. He pointed towards a house slightly further down on the opposite side of the road. "Do you know who lives there?"

"The Chaytor-Gills." The woman glanced up at him sharply. "Why are you asking? Is there anything wrong?"

Adrian had a feeling that she was a nosy neighbour who had suddenly realised that she might have stumbled on a source of juicy gossip. He decided to turn the tables and, while denying the woman's hopes, pick up some information that might help Lucy.

"No, they're not connected with our investigation," he said. "But as we passed, I noticed that an upstairs window was open, which seems odd when it's so cold, and the house has an empty look about it. We rang the doorbell, but there was no answer."

"Oh, she's there — well, she was, but she's out now. I happened to be looking through the window about an hour ago and I saw her friend — he's *always* around — pick her up in his Bentley. Mr Chaytor-Gill isn't here much, so he must work away." She frowned. "Come to think of it, I believe he has something to do with the police. I'm sure he's in some high-up position. Anyway, when Mr Chaytor-Gill *is* home, Mr Bentley — I don't know his real name, so that's what I call him because of his car — often comes with another woman, who I guess is his wife. They might all be friends, but the thing is, the other lady never comes with Mr B when Mr Chaytor-Gill is away." She gave them a significant look.

"Ooh!" Lucy said. "Do you think Mrs Bentley knows what's going on?"

"That I can't say, but," the woman lowered her voice, although there was no one nearby, "what I *do* know is that often, after Mr B picks Mrs C-G up, she's away for a couple of days." She paused. "And nights. Sometimes, when Mr Chaytor-Gill is away, Mr Bentley calls and his car is parked outside her house *all night*. I just happen to notice these things when I open and shut the curtains."

"Oh yes, there's something going on there all right." Lucy nodded sagely.

Adrian cleared his throat. "Well, time for us to go. Mrs . . . ?"

"Green," she said.

"Mrs Green. It's been nice talking to you. Our apologies for sitting on your wall to rest our flat feet."

"You're welcome." She was smiling now, friendly again.

Adrian pulled out his notebook, scribbled something in it and tore out the page. "What I'll do is leave your neighbours a note pointing out the dangers of leaving windows open."

"Quite right," said Mrs Green, turning to go back indoors. "It's an open invitation to burglars."

Lucy and Adrian dropped the note through the Chaytor-Gills' letterbox on their way back to their car, parked at the end of the cul-de-sac.

As they left, they drove past number four and waved to Mrs Green, who happened to be looking out of the lounge window.

* * *

Blade didn't linger in London. After the abrupt termination of his visit to Wriggley, he took the Tube to Paddington, where he had an early lunch before boarding a train back to Reading. He was back in Bramshill by 1.30 p.m., where John Hyde met him.

"Where is everyone?" he enquired. The incident room was deserted, apart from one constable.

"The civilians must still be at lunch, sir. They take a break at one o'clock," Hyde said.

"And the team? Are they all at lunch, too?"

"No. They're out." Hyde could not hide his pleased smirk as he added importantly, "I've given them all jobs to do."

"Jobs?"

"Can we go to your office, boss? Quite a lot happening. Things to show you. Thought I should get things moving quickly. New suspects." Hyde sounded excited.

"Suspects?"

"You'll see, boss. I'll explain." He led the way to Blade's desk. "The commandant brought this in." Hyde picked up the large brown envelope and handed it over.

Blade opened it and sat down to study the photograph. "So?"

"Well . . ." Hyde shifted uncomfortably, transferring his weight from one foot to the other. "I remembered what we discussed last night, sir, that there might be two murderers."

"Go on."

"And I, er, noticed *two* people in that photograph — Mrs Chaytor-Gill and Mr Dumble — who are both very familiar with Bramshill. So they probably knew Ashington too . . . I thought perhaps we should check them out."

"Check?" Blade spoke almost in a whisper. He seemed to be getting a headache too, because he held a hand to his forehead.

"Very discreetly, of course. I stressed the importance of that."

"Discreetly." Blade winced. Hyde wondered if his chief was starting a migraine.

"That's right. Discreetly. I told Headley and Robinson to start a check on Mr Dumble and sent Lucy Ramsey to see what she could find out about Mrs Chaytor-Gill. Oh, I nearly forgot, I think Adrian Harper might have gone with her."

Blade sat bolt upright but he remained silent while his sergeant told him about Adrian's astonishing recovery.

"I told him not to go out, I actually ordered him to go home, but I don't think he was taking much notice. Right, well, I think that brings you up to date, sir. Except," he added smugly, "I had the pictures of the two new suspects—" He caught Blade's expression. "*Possible witnesses* blown up and I've added them to the board."

"Have you now. And my son's? He's in this photo too," Blade said softly.

"Of course not, boss. I was particularly careful not to mention or identify him to the others."

"Or the commandant's picture? Is that on the board?" His voice was still soft.

Hyde tittered. "Ha, no, I don't think he'd like that."

"And do you think he'll be happy about his wife's picture being stuck up there, together with that of his deputy's husband? Has he seen them?" Blade's voice now shook with suppressed anger.

The young sergeant gulped. "No, he hasn't been here since this morning."

"Then I suggest you remove them all. Now. Then contact the team. Tell them to go straight home. I want them in the conference room sharp at eight tomorrow morning. When you've done that, go home yourself."

After the chastened John Hyde had slunk away, Blade spent nearly two hours at his desk, reading his notes and occasionally making new ones before sitting for several minutes deep in thought.

For some days now, he had been certain he knew who was behind the killings, and now the motive was becoming clear. But he needed evidence to prove it. And that was the bloody trouble, he thought moodily — the elusive proof. He reached for the files containing his team's reports and began to read them again, just in case he'd missed something the first time.

He started at the very beginning with the cleaning ladies' statements. They produced nothing of value this time around either. His team had carefully noted the records in the security guards' hut at the entrance where all traffic and pedestrians were checked, but nothing significant was reported at the relevant times. The report observed that it would be easy for an intruder to bypass the barrier and access the grounds by walking through the woods. But no tyre tracks or fresh footprints had been found, and the fence was undamaged.

So far, so expected. Blade turned to Bill Headley's file and the report on the CCTV camera. "That's where the answer's hiding," he muttered to himself when he had finished reading. He stood up, stretched and without pausing to put on his anorak, stomped across to the security office where he questioned the two men on duty for half an hour before returning to his desk to complete his notes.

It was almost six o'clock before he finally, with a sense of dread, phoned his wife to say he was leaving for home.

CHAPTER FOURTEEN

JULIE BEGAN as soon as Blade opened the front door.

"Have you spoken to Dorothy?"

"No."

"Or Richard?"

He shook his head wearily, waiting for the coming onslaught.

Well, he's been on the phone to me twice, the poor boy. And do you know what that woman said to him?"

"No." *But I'm sure you're going to tell me.*

"She accused him of murder."

"I very much doubt that she would have—"

"She said he'd poisoned Harold Ashington."

"Oh, come on, she wouldn't have—"

"I thought she was so nice when she was here the other night, laughing and joking, accepting our hospitality. Bitch is too polite a word for her, the . . . the *cow*!" Blade almost smiled. "She said Richard had made cyanide in the university chemistry lab and had used it to kill that bastard Ashington."

"She was probably trying to tell him what people might *think* could have happened. My guess is that Dorothy was trying to help him strengthen his alibi. It is pretty weak, you know." *Like yours.*

"That's right. Make excuses for her. You're as bad as she is. He's your son, for God's sake. But you do nothing to help him. You're bloody pathetic."

Her voice was full of venom, her face red with fury. Blade had never seen Julie like this before. Her anger was like a tidal wave, carrying him along until he drowned in her contempt and disapproval.

Not daring to speak in case he antagonised her further, he shrugged off his anorak and pushed past her into the kitchen. He sat down at the table.

Still remonstrating bitterly, she followed him into the warmth. She took a plate from the warming drawer and, none too gently, set it down in front of him. Beef casserole. He looked down at his plate and then raised his eyes to Julie.

"Where's yours?"

"I've eaten."

"But it's only," he glanced at the wall clock, "five to seven."

"I know." She turned to go.

"Look, Julie, I know it's hard for you — and Richard. But I *am* making progress. I'll give Richard a call tonight. I will find the killer, I promise."

"That's what you said last night." She left the room, slamming the door behind her.

Blade fiddled with his dinner, prodding at the pieces of meat. He set his fork down, pushed the plate away and sat staring at it. Finally, he got to his feet and scraped the meal into the bin.

Moving into the sitting room, he was relieved to find it empty. He guessed Julie had gone to bed early in order to keep out of his way. He poured himself a stiff whisky and sat nursing the drink, pondering over the evidence gathered so far and thinking about his afternoon talk with the security men. His conversation with them had convinced him there could be only one logical answer to the problem that fitted all the known facts. And now he was sure he knew that answer.

He knew who was responsible for both murders.

The problem was proving it.

He refilled his glass, drained it quickly, topped it up again and thought about his earlier promise to Julie. He picked up the phone and called Richard.

"Hello, son."

From his slurred speech it seemed that Richard had been drinking too.

"Pish off, Dad."

Blade blinked and listened to the dialling tone with a slight smile. He wasn't angry at being cut off — if anything, he felt relieved. At least he was spared another furious tirade. He put down the phone, shuffled across the room, went upstairs and climbed into bed.

Julie had her back to him. She was pretending to be asleep. He turned and faced the other way.

* * *

Bob Fraser gave Dorothy a hug. "I thought you'd be late tonight. Have a good journey?"

She nodded. "It was snowing when I left Loughborough, so I feared the worst, but it soon eased, then stopped altogether. I thought I'd better call in at Bramshill to tell the boss how I got on with his precious son, but then I had a call from John Hyde telling me to go straight home. I've got to go in early in the morning though."

"Great! A nice long evening together. We mustn't waste it. Why don't we go to that little Italian place we discovered the other day — Antonio's, wasn't it? I've got the number, so I'll book a table. We can have a pizza, then came back and relax by the fire with a drink and watch telly," her husband paused, eyebrows raised, "or something."

The restaurant was almost empty, the weather had kept most people indoors, so there had been no need to book and they found a seat in a quiet corner. The pizzas were huge, the sides almost overlapping the large dinner plates. Dorothy gazed in wonder. "Just look at that! I'll never eat it all. You'd better ask for a box and I'll take half home."

"No need. I'll eat what you can't manage. So, how did you get on with Blade Junior?"

She grimaced. "He struck me as a spoilt little bugger. His mam and dad think the sun shines out of his backside, but I didn't like him. I did my best to get him to remember people or anything else that could place him clear of the murder scene at the relevant times, but he obviously wasn't even trying to think, as if he didn't much care." Dorothy paused. "But a killer? I really don't know." In broad Geordie, she added, "Ye can never tell what's going on in people's minds."

She nodded towards the wine bottle. "Come on, Bob lad, pay attention. Can ye not see, man? Me glass is empty."

* * *

"So, did you give those detective constables the runaround like you said you would," Becky asked, smiling.

"I certainly did," John Hyde replied. "I found jobs for them all. Sent them out on inquiries."

"So, Superintendent Blade must have been very pleased with you when he got back. Is that why he's given you almost a whole afternoon off?"

Hyde's face clouded and he sounded doubtful. "Mmm. He was in a rather strange mood. He didn't actually *say* he was pleased. He didn't say much at all really.".

His expression brightened. "But you're right. We've got almost a whole afternoon to ourselves. We mustn't waste it." He tilted his head and raised his eyebrows hopefully.

"That's exactly what I was thinking." Becky's gaze travelled to the stairs. "Did you hear the window rattling in the wind last night? It kept me awake. You can fix that first. Then the ironing board needs a screw in it, it wobbles all over the place. I told you we shouldn't buy second-hand. But don't you worry, we won't waste a minute of any precious time we're given. There are loads of jobs I can find for you."

CHAPTER FIFTEEN

SOME TIME before six, Julie felt Blade slowly ease himself out of bed, evidently anxious to avoid another confrontation. Carrying his clothes over one arm, he tiptoed to the bathroom.

Julie was already wide awake. She half sat, leaning on one arm, muttering, "That's it, slink out, you creep." Suddenly, like a little girl, she stuck out her tongue.

She took a deep breath and opened her mouth to call after him, but instead collapsed back onto the pillow, exhausted after her sleepless night. Her rancour towards her husband had grown, nurtured during the endless hours of darkness, during which she had been forced to listen to his regular breathing, punctuated by the occasional snore.

Did she really hate Ralph?

Only a week ago, such a possibility wouldn't have entered her head. Before the discovery of Ashington's corpse, they had been a normal, loving family.

And now?

Julie pushed the question away, unwilling to face the answer. Her body ached, stiff from the tension of all those long, dark hours. Her stomach remained knotted in anxiety — and fear.

She buried her face in the pillow, which soon became soaked with her tears.

* * *

After an invigorating shower and a quick breakfast of muesli, Ralph Blade was at his desk just after seven thirty. He left the office door open to get a view of the table in the conference room.

John Hyde was the first to arrive, smiling uncertainly at his boss. Blade gave no indication that he'd seen him.

Tony Robinson came in next, much to Hyde's relief. It gave him an excuse to move away from Blade's open door, as well as an opportunity to question the detective constable. Did he and Bill actually speak to Mr Keith Dumble yesterday?

Perspiration glistened on Hyde's brow.

Before Tony could reply, Bill Headley, Dorothy, Lucy and Adrian all entered together in a noisy group.

Dorothy took Hyde aside. "Is the boss in?"

"In his office."

"Come on then. He might want to see us before the conference."

She led the way. Hyde, following in her wake, mumbled, "I don't think he's in a very good mood."

But Dorothy didn't hear. She was already knocking lightly on the open door and going in.

"Good morning, sir," she said brightly.

Unsmiling, Blade nodded towards the chairs. As the two of them sat down, and without returning her greeting, he said brusquely, "You're not the flavour of the month in my household. My wife says you accused my son of poisoning Ashington. Then, when I tried to speak to the boy last night, he told me to piss off."

Dorothy wriggled uncomfortably, while John Hyde visibly brightened, relieved to find that the inspector, not himself, was the object of his chief's displeasure.

"And to cap it all," Blade grumbled, "the sergeant here has added the commandant's wife and his deputy's husband to our list of murder suspects. I dread to think what they'll say when they find out."

Hyde looked down, tense again.

"I didn't accuse your son—" Dorothy began, but Blade waved her to silence.

"I know," he said. "I'm guessing you were trying to help him see how things might look to others." She nodded vigorously. "But I've been thinking. We can't go on like this, hiding facts from the rest of the team."

He switched his attention to Hyde. "And as for your new suspects," Hyde held his breath, "you're quite right. We must be seen to probe every possibility thoroughly." Hyde exhaled noisily. "So I suggest—"

Blade was interrupted yet again, this time by a loud rendition of *Für Elise*. He fished his mobile from his pocket. "I must take this," he said. "Get the conference started and brief the team on my son's involvement. Give them all the facts. Hide nothing. Close the door on your way out."

He waited until they had gone before answering the call. "Good morning, sir."

"Are you alone? Can you talk?" Chief Superintendent Oliver asked without preamble.

"Yes."

"Are you getting anywhere with this business? Making any progress at all?"

"Well, it's only been four days and—"

"I'm aware of that, but the shit's hitting the fan here. The chief constable is under increasing pressure from the Met, who claim that since the victim, Harold Ashington, is one of theirs they should handle the case. My own view is that they want to take control to protect their reputation. I think there's more to this business than meets the eye. Local politics is involved."

Stan Oliver went on to tell Blade that the Home Office was taking a sudden unexplained interest in the case and asking the Yard questions they seemed unable to answer. The press were involved as well. A reporter from the *Record* had been spotted nosing around the Home Office, asking questions about the Ashington killing — although how the Home Office might be linked to the murders at the police college wasn't clear.

"Look, Ralph, I'm sorry to tell you this, but the chief's got to watch his own back too, you know. He's giving you two more days. If you haven't got any answers by then, he'll have to hand the case over to the Yard."

"Tell him I'll have cracked it by then," Blade said with a confidence he didn't feel. "Three days at the most."

He switched off the mobile and pocketed it. He took a quick look through the blind that covered the glass on the top half of the door and saw that there was an animated discussion going on around the conference table. Guessing that his own family was the subject, he decided to delay his entrance.

* * *

The detectives eyed each other uncomfortably during the shocked hush that followed the briefing, until Bill Healey, as the oldest member of the team, felt obliged to say something.

"Look, I've known the boss ever since he joined us from the Met. I've worked with him for years and watched him rise through the ranks — and he did it all by honest, hard graft. There's nothing bent about him, and I'd always trust him to do the right thing."

"Yeah, maybe you would," Robinson grumbled. "But this *isn't* the right thing. Going off to interview prime suspects himself and hiding vital facts from us, I ask you! His own family is involved in this case. They should be among the prime suspects in my opinion. And to top it all, he's got personal history with the murder victim. Yet he doesn't think we ought to know these things."

"He told me and Sergeant Hyde," Dorothy pointed out. "And he has the backing of the chief constable and Chief Superintendent Oliver."

"Maybe so, but I still think it's wrong. He shouldn't be handling the case, especially with his hands-on approach. His job is to—"

Headley cut him short. "His job is to solve crimes. He doesn't operate like most other investigating officers, who sit behind their desks sifting through the detectives' reports. He does that too, of course, but he takes on a lot of the legwork himself. And he gets results."

Robinson was prevented from replying when Blade finally emerged from his office. But the superintendent was again distracted when, through the window onto the corridor, he saw a familiar figure pass by. With a muttered apology, he hurried to the door and called out, "Fred!"

The pathologist, who was carrying a large cardboard box, turned to Blade and gave him a smile. "Hello, Ralph. Have you nailed the killer or killers yet?"

"Not yet. What are you doing here? Don't tell me you've been called in to examine another corpse. Two is enough."

Dr Stoker grinned. "No. I've come to clear some stuff out of the lab. It's a shame, but the place will never be used again, so I'm salvaging the things I can use elsewhere."

"The lab? I didn't know they had one here," Blade said.

"Oh yes, just like the real thing. Fully equipped — except for the bodies." The grin widened. "Maybe your villains were trying to make up for that deficiency. It didn't work though, their victims ended up on the slab in my official workplace."

Blade didn't smile. "And this full equipment. Did it include cyanide, by any chance?"

"Of course." Fred Stoker was suddenly serious. "It's useful to acquaint or reacquaint students with the distinctive smell." His eyes narrowed. "But if you're wondering if any of the poison is missing, the answer's no. I thought of that and checked as soon as the victims' cause of death was confirmed. The cyanide bottle was full. Untouched."

"You should still have informed me, Fred. The poison could have been extracted and the bottle topped up. We'd better test to see if the contents have been diluted, and have the container checked for fingerprints."

"It will be smothered in mine for a start, never mind those of the hundreds of students — mostly police personnel — who've handled it."

"All the same," Blade persisted, "it needs to be done."

"I'll have it bagged for you," the pathologist said stiffly.

"No, I'll collect it now. If you'll lead the way?

"It's not there."

"So where is it?" Blade demanded, alarmed.

Stoker shook the box he was carrying so that the contents clinked. "It's in here. I'm taking it to my own lab."

"Just put the box down and open the lid."

Puffing and panting and complaining bitterly about being late for a meeting, the doctor did as he was told, revealing a jumble of bottles, laboratory glassware and packs of rubber gloves. Blade extracted a pair of gloves and put them on.

"Which one is the cyanide?"

Silently, Stoker indicated a green bottle. Blade picked it up.

"Thank you, Fred. I'll let you know the result."

In silence, the pathologist bent to retrieve his load, glared at Blade and turned on his heel. He marched towards the door, the box chinking as each foot hit the floor.

Blade watched him go. Still thoughtful, he made his way back to the conference room. The team watched curiously while he placed the bottle on the table and peeled off the latex gloves.

"That," he announced, "is a bottle of cyanide."

They listened attentively while he recounted his conversation with Fred Stoker. When he had finished, he turned to Hyde. "John, I want you to get this cyanide analysed. See if it's been diluted or if there's anything else unusual about it. And check the bottle for prints. Don't take it to our pathologist's lab, you'd better get it done in Woking, which should mitigate any chance of interference.

"Right, sir," said Hyde, adding hesitantly, "You don't think Dr Stoker—"

"I don't know what to think, John," his chief cut in. "I just want to cover all the angles. Bill," he switched his gaze to Headley, "take another look at that CCTV film. This time pay particular attention to what happens after the arrival of Dr Stoker. Apart from the patrol car men, he was the first official on the scene. He knows the importance of forensics — in fact he often points out vital clues."

Blade added, speaking deliberately, "The scarcity of evidence concerning both murders, plus the attacks on a suspect, Inspector Liddell, and our own PC Harper," he nodded towards Adrian, "are among the more puzzling aspects of this case."

"Yes, sir," Detective Constable Robinson said, "but I don't see why suspicion should be directed solely at Dr Stoker. After all, CID officers are just as aware of the importance of forensics. They're also just as capable of hiding or altering evidence, often with similar opportunities to do so."

He stared defiantly at Blade, while, during the brief silence that followed, his colleagues fiddled and wriggled in embarrassment.

Blade gave a wry smile. "I see where you're coming from, Tony." He looked around at the rest of the team. "I know you've all been told about my own family's link with this case, so," he clapped his hands, "what's the verdict?"

"We're all with you, sir," Dorothy said at once. "We're confident that if anything, er, *prejudicial* were to be uncovered you'd, er, um, do the right thing."

"And is that the verdict of you all?"

"Yes," the team chorused, apart from Tony Robinson, who stayed silent for a few breathless seconds. The others stared at him. Eventually, he answered with an almost imperceptible nod.

"Good. So, let's get on." With a significant glance at Robinson, Blade said, "John, when you've got the cyanide test underway, I want you to run a check on Dr Stoker."

Blade then briefly reiterated the results of the inquiries so far "Don't forget the character of the first victim, Ashington. He was a nasty piece of work, known to use blackmail to get what he wanted, but that doesn't give anyone the right to kill him. So, if he was up to his old tricks and we can identify his prey, we might get a result. I understand that Sergeant Hyde gave you all tasks to do yesterday after new evidence was handed in. He believes that everyone — no matter how high and mighty or how remotely connected to these murders — must be investigated thoroughly. He's right, of course, so I want you, Tony," he nodded at Robinson, "to continue what you and Bill started on yesterday. Find out anything you can about Mr Keith Dumble. Better still, interview him if you can track him down. Tell him we're in possession of a photograph showing him with the murdered man — you could show him a print — and take it from there. You'll be on your own this time because Bill will be busy watching his favourite CCTV programme." Bill Headley pulled a face.

Blade turned to Hyde. "John, regarding the inquiry into our Dr Stoker. I know he was in London before he came to us and did a lot of work for the Met, so your new friends at the Yard might be able to help you there. See if you can dig up any connection between him and Ashington."

He turned his attention to PC Ramsay. "What I said to Tony applies to you too, Lucy. I believe you were checking on the commandant's wife yesterday, so carry on. Tell her about the photograph. Take a copy with you and ask how well she knew Ashington, whether she noticed anything unusual and so on. Keep her talking, she might have important information without realising it."

Adrian put his hand up. "Sir!"

"Ah, PC Harper," Blade said genially. "Welcome back. It's good to see you on your feet again, up and running. I didn't expect the medics to sign you off so soon."

"Well, er, they haven't actually . . ."

"What the hell do you think you're doing, Constable?" Blade's genial smile was gone. "Go home. Now. You're not supposed to be here unless the doctors say you're well enough. I thought Sergeant Hyde made that clear to you yesterday."

Adrian attempted a grin. "Yes, sir. But I was bored, so Lucy let me go with her, just for the drive. We had a look at the road where the commandant lives—"

"You did *what*? For heaven's sake, man, you have a head injury. You were supposed to be off sick, possibly concussed. What if you'd dropped dead? The lawyers would have had a field day with that, wouldn't they? I'd have allowed you to work illegally. The compensation could have cost the police millions."

"Yes, sir. But the point is, we met a woman who gave us some information that could be useful because she—"

Blade put his head in his hands. The young constable's voice faltered but, bravely, he forged ahead. "She seemed to think Mrs Chaytor-Gill is having an affair with — well, she doesn't know Mr Dumble's name. She calls him 'Mr Bentley' because he always turns up in a Bentley car."

"Mr Dumble has a Bentley, sir." Bill Headley said.

Blade raised his head. "Oh, does he now?" He kept looking at Adrian. "So what else did your lady friend have to say?"

His anger apparently gone, Blade listened carefully while between them, Adrian and Lucy related what Mrs Green had told them. Bill Headley then reported on his and Tony's investigation into Mr Dumble, husband to Bramshill's deputy commandant.

It turned out that Mr Keith Dumble came from a privileged background — public school education and a chemistry degree from Cambridge. Now, at forty-four, his father having recently retired, he was managing director of the family chemical factory, located in an industrial park near

Basingstoke. He lived in a large, thatched cottage near the village of Lower Wield.

"There's a security guard posted at the factory gate. We showed him our cards and had a quiet word, warning him to be extra vigilant because there had been a spate of thefts of drugs from doctors' surgeries in the area. Afterwards we chatted a bit, and he mentioned that the boss, Mr Dumble, was in his office as usual, and pointed out his car — a Bentley."

Blade stroked his chin thoughtfully. "Well, we certainly need to interview Mr Dumble and Mrs Chaytor-Gill. Tony, try the factory first. If he's not there, go to his house. Lucy, if the commandant's wife isn't at home, you could pop over to Mr Dumble's place as well." He smiled. "You never know, you might find the pair of them together. Don't phone ahead to fix an appointment." He nodded to Robinson. "That applies to you too, Tony. Try and take them by surprise so they don't have time to get their stories straight — if indeed they do have anything to hide. But we mustn't forget that we're also investigating the murder of Roger Cotter, Bramshill's security chief. I've been working on that myself. I'm seeing his widow again today. We'll have another conference this evening."

The team exchanged glum looks. It was going to be another long day.

Blade stood up and clapped his hands together. "Off you go. I want you all back here with your reports at six o'clock." He pointed to Adrian. "Except you. Home. Now! I don't want to see you again until you're fully fit."

With a scraping of chairs the detectives got up to leave. Blade marched towards his office, calling over his shoulder, "A word, please, Inspector."

* * *

Blade got straight to the point.

"Chief Superintendent Oliver tells me a *Record* reporter has been nosing around in the Home Office asking questions about people connected to our investigation." He leaned forward and glared at Dorothy. "So, what can you tell me about that?"

Dorothy glared straight back. "Okay, I'll tell you. It was my husband, Bob. I told him to 'nose about', as you put it. He did it for me, not for the paper, not yet anyway."

Blade leaned back, staring at her in disbelief. "Just what do you think you're playing at?"

"It's worked fine in previous cases. People who won't speak to the police often talk to him. He gets the information I want, then, when the time's right, I give him the story, so he has a head start on the other papers."

Blade was aghast. "You can't do that."

"Look, *sir*, don't start lecturing me about rules and regulations because, from what I've heard, you shouldn't have been given this case from the start. I've also heard that you use unconventional methods. You keep your ideas close to your chest, telling no one, while you work things out and come up with the right solution. Well, I've got *my* methods, and *I* get results too. I'm working on my own ideas about this case and I'm not ready to discuss them with you yet, not until I'm sure you won't be able to laugh them out of court."

His face red, Blade shook his head slowly. His shoulders drooped. "The way things are going, Detective Inspector Fraser, I won't be surprised if I land up *in* court. But let's press on and try to wrap this case up before that happens. In the meantime — before you solve the case using your own *unconventional* methods — you'd better clear up the mess you've created at the Home Office. That's your job for the day. Get along there now and soothe any toes that have been trodden on."

Dorothy's face brightened. "Really! Do you trust me not to step on a few *more* toes?"

"Get out!" he shouted. Then, as she opened the door, he added quietly, "See what else you can find out. But this time tell *me* about it." He summoned a tired grin. "I take your point about us both having our own methods. Maybe it's time we worked together."

"Right, boss."

Smiling, she closed the door gently behind her.

CHAPTER SIXTEEN

"I'LL DROP you off on the way," said Lucy, opening the car door.

"No need . . . Ow!"

"And mind your thick head on the roof."

"It's out of your way," Adrian said.

"No it isn't. I want to call in at the hospital to get the latest on Angela Liddell. I'm supposed to check every day."

"In any case, there's still no need to take me home, because I'm coming with you."

"No, you're not. You heard what the man said." Lucy folded her arms.

"Just for the ride if anyone asks. They can't stop me from—"

"I said 'No'."

The rest of the fifteen-minute drive passed in stony silence. Finally, Lucy steered the Clio into the three-bed semi that Adrian shared with his mother. "You might as well come in and see Mum," he said. "She wants to meet you."

"Oh? You've been talking about me then. So, what have you told her?"

He wriggled uncomfortably in his seat. "Nothing. Just that we work together and all that."

"And all what?"

"And that I thought you were quite nice and—"

"Quite nice. _Quite nice?_"

"So, why don't you come in and let her see for herself what a nagging old dragon you _really_ are."

"I haven't got time," she said.

"Yes, you have. I'll check on Angela Liddell for you and let the boss know how she is. He can't stop me from calling in to see a fellow patient. Come on."

Suddenly nervous, Lucy got out of the car and followed him up the path to the front door. Grinning, he unlocked the door, opened it and gave her a gentle push. "I hope you're ready. Third degree coming up!"

Before she could reply, a door at the far end of the dark passage opened, simultaneously releasing bright light, a delicious smell of baking and Mrs Harper into the hallway.

"I heard that, Adrian," his mother said, wagging a finger at him. "That was very rude. Third degree indeed. You'll frighten the poor girl." She wiped her hand on her apron and held it out. "You must be Lucy."

"That's me," Lucy answered, smiling. She took the hand in both of hers, wondering how such a tiny woman could have given birth to such a huge son.

And tiny she was. Lucy thought she mustn't be much more than four feet tall. Her skin was as smooth as that of a teenager and like a teenager, she wore her hair long. Only the crows' feet around her eyes betrayed her true age. She had one of those faces that people call ugly-beautiful. It was certainly a cheerful face, with a wide, generous smile.

"I'll put the kettle on. Do you prefer tea or coffee?" she asked, leading the way back to the kitchen."

"I really don't have time to—"

"Yes, she does," Adrian said. "I'm doing the hospital visit for her, so she'll have time for a cuppa."

"Oh." His mother looked annoyed. "You're going out again?" She turned to Lucy. "I've been given time off work to look after him, but he's never in. Silly boy. Dangerous job, dangerous sports . . . He's always getting injured playing rugby. Just like his father. He was a policeman too, but I suppose you know that. And look what happened to him — killed falling off a mountain while Adrian was still a babe in arms. No wonder I worry!"

She smiled at her visitor. "So, what's it to be, my dear? Tea or coffee? And the chocolate cake's just ready, can you smell it? It's Adrian's favourite. You must have a slice. I'll give you the recipe. Are you a good cook yourself?"

"There you are, I told you so," Adrian said, grinning. "The third degree has started." All three of them laughed.

Politely declining the proffered seat, Lucy drank her coffee and ate her cake standing up. "That was lovely, Mrs Harper, but I really must be off. Another time perhaps, and I'd love to have that recipe."

Adrian escorted Lucy to the car and opened the door for her. "There, that wasn't so bad, was it? I reckon you passed the test with flying colours."

"Test?"

"Yeah. I don't know if you're aware of this, but us chaps are born to one of just two categories of mother — first, those who believe that no woman on earth is good enough for their precious sons, and, second, those — like mum — who have to feel sure that any prospective wife is capable of looking after—"

"Hang on a minute! Did I miss something there?" Lucy turned the ignition key. "I don't recall you proposing marriage. When did that happen?" Her tone was frostier than the weather.

Adrian just had time to notice how attractive she was with that glow on her cheeks before he was forced to leap clear of the wheels. They spun for a few seconds, scattering shards of ice, and then, with a painful grating of gears, Lucy pulled away.

"What was all that about?" Adrian wondered out loud. He scratched his head and winced.

* * *

The ward sister looked up from her paperwork and smiled when she saw Adrian in the office doorway. She beckoned him in.

"How's that fat head of yours? Still fixed to your shoulders, I see."

He grinned. "Yeah, they'll have to try harder than that if they want to knock it off. I've come to see my fellow casualty. Is she any better?"

The sister nodded. "Angela Liddell? Yes, she regained consciousness last night. A tough cookie that one. The first thing she did was demand something to eat. She hasn't had anything yet, just fluids. The doctor will have to have a look at her first. He's on his rounds now."

"Can I see her?"

"Yes, and then you can have a word with the consultant while he's here. She's in one of the two singles — next door to the one you were in, not the open ward." The sister gave a wicked smile. "It's usually that pretty policewoman — the one that used to come and hold your hand — that checks on Miss Liddell. Is she off today?" She winked. "I think she's sweet on you. Play your cards right and—"

"I think you could be wrong there, Sister," Adrian said. "I don't know what I'm supposed to have done, but she's not at all pleased with me just now."

He left the office, still shaking his head. The swing doors to the adjacent ward were open and he headed for the central desk, where two young nurses, one white, one black, were studying the patients' reports. They looked up, both smiling broadly, and chorused,

"Hello! Can't keep away, eh?"

"Have you come to see us?"

"Does what's-her-name who used to come and visit you — Lucy is it? — know about this?"

"Well, we won't tell her."

They subsided in a fit of giggles. "Sorry, ladies," Adrian said grinning, "another time perhaps. I've come to visit Miss Liddell. I hear she's woken up at last."

They both raised their eyes to the ceiling. "*Hear* is about right," the black nurse said. "The night staff told us she came to just before five this morning and she's been making a helluva noise ever since, keeps complaining that she's hungry. The doctor is with her now," she glanced towards the end of the open ward and the two en suite rooms he and Angela Liddell had occupied. "Oh, here he comes. You can have a word. You already know him, of course."

A shortish portly figure emerged from one of the rooms. He was pale with strands of hair swept across his balding crown. He looked nothing like a doctor. Only the stethoscope hanging around his neck proclaimed him as such. Followed by a gaggle of young women holding clipboards, he marched through the ward, bestowing gracious smiles upon the patients as he went. He made straight for the nurses' station, the smile broadening into a wide grin as he approached.

"I thought we'd got rid of you," he said, vigorously pumping Adrian's hand. "Can't keep away, eh?"

"It's good to see you again, Dr Handley. I'd like to thank you for all you did for me."

The doctor gave a dismissive wave. "All part of the service, dear boy."

"Actually, I'm here to see Miss Liddell. Would it be all right if I popped in?"

The doctor took a step back, forcing his team to jolt against one another. Eyes twinkling, he looked at Adrian apprehensively. "We-ell, do you really feel up to it? Go ahead if you think you're brave enough — you never know, she might even be pleased to see you — but be warned, that is a very angry young lady in there. She might well eat you alive." He turned to the nurses. "Oh, that reminds me, would you organise some breakfast for her, please? She's threatening to die of starvation." He shook his head in wonder. "It's hard to believe she's thinking about food so soon. That was a vicious attack. She must be extremely fit."

Adrian nodded. "Yes, she is. She goes for long early morning runs, even when it's snowing. And, um, talking about fitness, I feel fine now, doctor, so I was wondering if you could sign me off as being okay to work?"

"Good heavens, man! It's damned cold out there. Why don't you just relax and put your feet up by the fire while you have the chance? But it's not up to me. I've signed you over to your GP, so you'll have to ask him. And now I must get on." Dr Handley glanced at his entourage. "Come along, ladies, let's see to the rest of our patients."

While the team trooped over to the nearest bed, Adrian smiled at the nurses somewhat apprehensively, and turned to face the ordeal of the walk through the open ward. Avoiding looking at the occupants, some of whom were uncovered, he headed for Angela Liddell's room, conscious that the eyes of every single woman in the ward were following his progress.

He tapped on the door and stepped inside. Like the women on the ward outside, Angela too was staring at him. But there was no hint of curiosity in her gaze.

Instead, she wore a look of undisguised animosity.

"I know you," she said with no trace of friendliness in her voice. "I've seen you before."

Adrian moved towards her, risking a half-smile. "I'm PC Adrian Harper and I—"

"That's it!" she exclaimed. "That's where it was. You were with that bunch of idiots in that so-called incident room when I saw my picture on the board."

"That's right, Angela. May I call you Angela?"

"No, you bloody can't, Constable. It's Inspector Liddell to you."

"Insp—"

"Or, even better, ma'am."

"I just came to see how you're getting on, erm, ma'am," Adrian said patiently, dragging a chair across to her bedside. "Although this is a women's ward, I was put in the room next to yours because it had the only other spare bed in the hospital."

"Bed?" Angela said and her eyes widened as the memory of the night of her attack returned. "That's right. You were on my bed. I saw your face in the light from the corridor. I was being attacked . . . A man wearing a hood . . ." She held out her hands and looked in wonder at her bandaged wrist. "And you came in and tried to stop him but—" she paused again, frowning, "but there was someone else there, they coshed you." She shook her head. "After that, I can't remember a thing."

"That makes two of us," Adrian muttered with feeling.

"But what were you doing there? It was the middle of the night. How did you come to be in my room?"

"I heard you scream." Adrian paused. "I happened to be next door, so I rushed in to help."

"You just happened to be . . ." She opened her eyes wide. "You were bloody watching me! I remember now. Your lot think I killed that security man, the one I found dead in my room, so you were spying on me in case I ran away."

"Guarding you," Adrian lied, recalling Blade's instructions. *See that Inspector Liddell doesn't do a runner.* "And a good job too, in view of what happened."

"Good job? *Good job*! I don't call that good. They bloody clobbered you — and look at the state of me. I could have been killed if—"

"You *would* have been killed if I hadn't stopped them," Adrian interrupted, piqued. "That's why they were there. We believe their plan was to cut your wrists to make it look like suicide. When I surprised them and tackled the one on your bed they panicked and clubbed you, leaving you for dead." He paused. "Ma'am."

"Oh," she said quietly. She looked abashed. She held her bandaged wrist up and studied it again.

"So," Adrian said, "what we want to know is, did you see their faces, or notice anything else that might give us a clue as to their identities?"

She thought for a moment, started to shake her head and stopped, wincing. "The light was poor, as you know, and they were both wearing dark hoodies, either black or navy blue. But it was all over so quickly. I'm sorry."

Adrian nodded sympathetically. "I know what you mean. It was the same for me. I didn't even see the one that," he gave a slight smile, "clobbered me."

"I shouldn't have said that," she acknowledged. "Forgive me. I've been railing on at you, giving you a hard time, when really I should be thanking you for saving my life. So, thank you! I really am very grateful. And of course you can call me Angela." She fluttered her eyelashes and added demurely, "I'll even let you shorten it to Angie if you arrange for someone to feed me. I'm bloody starving."

"I guess the whole hospital knows about your hunger, ma'am." His smile widened. "I think I'd better stick to 'ma'am', ma'am. The good news is that your breakfast is on its way. I heard the doc order it for you. And here it comes." The door opened to admit a nurse carrying a tray.

Adrian stood up, bid Angela farewell, and once more braved the stares of the patients.

CHAPTER SEVENTEEN

IN THE rear-view mirror, Lucy watched the figure of the downcast Adrian grow smaller until it finally disappeared from sight. Her annoyance was soon overtaken by a stronger emotion: Worry.

Despite her ambition to be a detective, she was as yet a rookie police constable. So, how should she handle the interview with Mrs Chaytor-Gill, someone with connections to the highest echelons of the police service? Obviously, Blade was expecting Lucy to ask personal, and possibly embarrassing, questions of this woman.

Her anxiety grew with every mile, reaching its peak as she turned into Oak Grove, where she spotted Mrs Green peeping through her sitting-room window. Taking a deep breath, she drew up outside the Chaytor-Gills' upmarket home.

There was no one in.

Relieved, Lucy returned to the car, reset the satnav and turned to leave. As she passed, she detected a movement in a garden on the opposite side of the road and gave a loud toot, laughing when Mrs Green jumped in alarm. The nosy neighbour had left her cosy sitting room for a better view of the action and had been peeping around a snow-covered bush.

Her relief at not having to interview Mrs Chaytor-Gill was short-lived, her anxiety returning with added strength the nearer she drew to Keith Dumble's residence. The satnav directed her through rolling countryside — the patchwork of woods and arable fields now blanketed in snow — to the village of Lower Wield.

As soon as she pulled into the kerb, she gave a sigh of relief. Another car was approaching from the opposite direction. The two cars parked bonnet to bonnet and the drivers got out, smiling at each other.

"I was hoping I'd see you," said Lucy to Tony Robinson. "Mrs Chaytor-Gill wasn't at home so, as the boss suggested, I came here."

"And I'm here because Mr Dumble wasn't at the factory," said Tony. "So, let's join forces." He laughed. "You never know, we might catch them at it."

Lucy drew a woolly hat from her anorak pocket and pulled it down over her ears. They walked up to the entrance in silence. There was no traffic in this secluded lane. There didn't seem to be any birds either. The only sound breaking the almost unearthly hush was the snow crunching beneath their feet.

They paused outside a pair of open double iron gates set in a tall, well-tailored hedge.

"Ooh! Look at that. What a picture." Lucy spoke in an awed whisper. "Isn't it lovely. Just imagine what it must be like in the summer, with the trees in their greenery, the lawns and flower beds. Oh! And the house. Just look at it. It's like a picture book."

"Yeah," Robinson replied unenthusiastically, sparing only a casual glance for the thatched roof, leaded windows and half-timbered architecture. "No sign of our Mr Dumble's Bentley. It's probably tucked up in that double garage. But the Renault parked outside the front door," he inspected the thick layer of snow that covered the roof and windscreen of the Mégane, "looks as though it's been there all night. See? No new tyre tracks. Come on, let's get out of the cold. I'll bet it's nice and warm in there."

Leaving a trail of footprints, they approached the front door. Lucy noted the dormant wisteria that covered the thatched porch and pictured the fragrant, violet-blue flowers that would bloom in May and June. She refrained from further exclamations, as her companion obviously had no feeling for beautiful gardens.

Tony rang the bell. He glanced down at her and said quietly, "It'll be better if we can interview them separately, so each doesn't know what the other one says and—"

Lucy gave him a quick nod of understanding as the heavy oak door was opened by a woman who, despite the cold, was wearing a white blouse and floral cotton skirt. With a tentative half-smile, she looked from one to the other of them, her eyebrows raised in inquiry.

"Good morning, Mrs Chaytor-Gill. We are—" But Tony was again cut short.

"What do you want? How do you know my name?" She stared at him, the slight smile gone, the voice peremptory.

He produced his warrant card. "I'm Detective Constable Anthony Robinson and this is Constable Ramsay." Lucy held up her own card. "We are part of the team investigating the murder of Chief Superintendent Harold Ashington. We believe you were acquainted with the gentleman, ma'am, and might be able to help us with our inquiries."

"You're quite wrong. I can't help you. I know who you mean, of course, but I didn't *know* him."

"Who is it, Anthea?" someone called from inside the house. "What's going on?"

"The police," she shouted over her shoulder. "Something to do with the Bramshill murder."

A man, casually dressed in polo shirt and well-worn corduroy trousers, appeared at her side, frowning.

"You'd better come in," he said testily. "And shut the door behind you. You're letting the cold in."

He led the way into a large half-timbered sitting room complete with traditional oak beams and huge inglenook fireplace. But there, tradition ended. The fire that blazed in

144

a double wood-burning stove was backed up by radiators on three walls.

Lucy was disappointed. Where were the chintzy curtains, sofas and armchairs? All the furnishing was 'modern' — two large white leather settees and four matching chairs with black velvet cushions. Floor-length drapes hung at the windows — black, with a white heron motif. The original beams in the ceiling had been painted white and the deep pile carpet was black with a zigzagging white pattern.

Outraged, she glanced through a wide archway and spotted — yes — a huge kitchen-diner. She guessed that two, perhaps even three, rooms had been knocked into one to accommodate it. Here, the black and white theme changed to grey with shiny metal. She was surprised to note that the old stone floor had been retained, probably because it was grey. How could someone vandalise what must have been a charming old cottage to create this hideous monstrosity?

She glanced at her colleague to see his reaction. But Tony seemed unconcerned. She reflected ruefully that his earlier guess that it would be "nice and warm in there" was accurate but their reception was decidedly chilly.

"What's this all about?" Keith Dumble demanded peevishly. "You can't seriously think we have anything to do with the Bramshill deaths."

"Does my husband know you're here?" Anthea added, equally testy. "You *do* know who he is, I presume."

"Of course, ma'am," Robinson said politely. "He's naturally very interested in the case and has been most helpful to us. As a matter of fact, it's because your husband gave us this," he fished in his anorak pocket, pulled out an envelope and handed it to her, "that we've come here to see you today."

Mrs Chaytor-Gill frowned, drawing out the photograph. "That's us! Look, Keith." Dumble moved to look over her shoulder. "It must have been taken at Bramshill's open day. Yes, I remember now, the official photographer followed us around for a while. There we are with Roderick, Felicity and

Mr Ashington, the man who was murdered. I don't know the young man, we weren't introduced, but I thought he might be Mr Ashington's son."

"He isn't, but we are aware of his identity," Tony said. "We're having a word with everyone in the picture — indeed, anyone who knew the victim — in the hope—"

"I told you, I didn't *know* him," Anthea interrupted. Her tone was icy.

"Or had any contact with him, socially or otherwise, in the hope that they might recall something that might be helpful to us," Tony continued. "I'm sure that your husband, with his long and distinguished connection with the police service, would understand that, which is possibly why he gave us this photo."

"Well, I can't remember anything about the man."

"Hmm, well, why not have a word with Constable Ramsay? It's surprising how sometimes an innocuous remark can trigger a buried memory. Meanwhile, I'll just have a quick word with Mr Dumble."

Tony Robinson shot a glance at her companion, who, looking startled, gave a slight nod.

Enthusiastically, Lucy added, "Ooh, yes, and perhaps, while we chat, Mrs Chaytor-Gill might let me see some more of this lovely cottage. I can see a fantastic kitchen through there." She gestured towards the wide archway.

Looking surprised, Anthea invited her unwanted visitor to precede her into the kitchen-diner. As soon as they were inside, she looked at Lucy in amazement. "You mean you *like* it?"

"Oh, yes, I think it's just, erm, just . . ." Lucy couldn't think what to say.

"Well, I *hate* it."

The two women stared at each other until, suddenly, they both broke into laughter.

The ice had been broken.

"I was just trying to be polite," Lucy explained. "It's not really to my taste at all."

146

"Nor mine. This is Felicity's style. But upstairs has been left unspoilt. Do you want to see?"

"Yes, please."

There were four bedrooms, three with fireplaces, plus a bathroom. The master bedroom had had the most done to it. An en-suite shower-room had been built into one corner, but, apart from the central heating, no other alterations had been made. The floor even sloped in places and some of the boards creaked.

Lucy took it all in, noting how cosy and comfortable the master bedroom was. The double bed was unmade, and she saw a crumpled nightdress on one side and a pair of pyjamas casually discarded on the other.

Now she wouldn't have to ask any embarrassing personal questions. The evidence was there, in front of her eyes. A quick peek into the en suite revealed two sets of used bath and hand towels, a pair of earrings on the windowsill.

"I know what you're doing and what you're thinking." Mrs Chaytor-Gill was watching her with evident amusement. "Over the years I've learned a lot about police work — inevitable really. My husband used to talk a lot about The Job." Anthea nodded towards a chaise-longue at the foot of the bed. "Let's sit and chat, as your partner suggested. And for heaven's sake, take that anorak off. You must be baking in here."

Lucy complied with a relieved grin, fishing in the pocket for her notebook. "Thank you, it is rather warm. Do you mind if I make notes?" Anthea shook her head.

They settled on the couch. "All I ask is that you treat what I tell you with discretion," Anthea said. "My guess is that you're all wondering about the nature of our relationship — the Chaytor-Gills and the Dumbles, that is." She paused, seeming to gather her thoughts. "We didn't know each other until Felicity Dumble got the job as my husband's deputy. We began to socialise, and it soon became apparent that Felicity and my husband were becoming more than just good friends. Naturally, Keith and I were concerned. We met a number of times to console each other and discuss what to do, and — surprise — ended up falling for each other." She gave a short laugh. "What to do? Well, to cut a long story short, the four of us have decided simply to swap partners — after quick and, hopefully, quiet divorces. But there's a snag. As you know, the police college is closing and both Roderick and Felicity will be out of work. The problem is this: There is the possibility of a really good job for Roderick, and later perhaps another in the same organisation for Felicity. But any hint of scandal would scupper their chances — the applicants must be squeaky clean. For obvious reasons I can't go into details or reveal the nature of the job. Anyway, we've decided to keep the divorces on hold until the employment situation is clear." Anthea gave a small conspiratorial smile. "So, I hope you can persuade your Superintendent Blade not to make what I've told you public. I assure you it can't have anything to do with the murder."

* * *

Downstairs, the atmosphere was distinctly chilly, with none of the cordiality that was developing between the two women.

For a start there was no invitation for Tony Robinson to remove his anorak and take a seat. He did so anyway, carefully placing the garment on a settee and sitting beside it, his notebook on his knee.

That was a mistake. Dumble remained standing, looking down at his unwelcome visitor, in control.

He nodded towards the notebook. "I don't know what you'll find to write in that. You heard what Mrs Chaytor-Gill said. We don't know the people in that photograph. I'd never met any of them before and I haven't seen them since. We were introduced, of course, but I can't even remember their names. So, if that's all . . ."

"You're not a regular visitor to Bramshill, sir?" Tony asked.

"Certainly not. Why should I be? My wife happens to work there, that's all. It was the open day. I was there to

148

support her," he paused, "and, perhaps, to satisfy my own curiosity."

Tony nodded enthusiastically. "Yes, I see that, sir — an insight into the workings of the police service and how the senior officers are trained. Quite a different world to your own, eh? I understand you own a chemical works."

"That's right. I run the laboratory and factory that my father founded sixty years ago. He retired recently."

"Oh wow!" Tony looked impressed. "You must have had to study hard to qualify for a job like that."

"I have a degree in chemistry, yes."

Tony scribbled in his notebook, tongue protruding from the corner of his mouth. When he'd finished writing, he leaned back, looked up at his unwilling host and asked, all innocence, "And does your factory produce cyanide, sir?"

Dumble stiffened. "What sort of question is that?" he snapped. "What are you implying?"

"I'm not implying anything, sir. It's just that I was reading about potassium cyanide the other night and I wondered what it was used for industrially. I thought that since I'm here, you'd be the best person to tell me."

"Among other things, it's used in gold mining and the process of electroplating," was the short reply.

"Well I never! Who'd have thought? And another thing I learned in this article — it was about making suicide pills for spies during World War Two — is that cyanide is a crystalline salt that looks like sugar and is highly soluble in water," Tony gave a tiny, mischievous smile, "or whisky."

"Enough!" Keith Dumble thundered. "I must ask you and your companion to leave. I'm not answering any more of your damned impertinent questions, and I'm warning you now that I'm making an official complaint about you." He turned to face Anthea and Lucy, who had hurried downstairs at the sound of his raised voice. "This damned idiot has just accused me not only of poisoning that copper in Bramshill, but also of making the bloody cyanide to do it."

"I've done no such thing," Tony protested. "I was simply—"

Anthea, an anxious expression on her face, waved him to silence. "Just do as he says. Go."

She gripped Lucy's arm. "Get him out of here. I'll call you after I've calmed Keith down. Have you got a number I can ring?"

"Here. My mobile number's on it." Lucy, who had already put her anorak on, took a card out of her bag and handed it over.

Seconds later, she and Tony were back outside in the cold.

"Huh. Fine pair they are," Tony grumbled, still struggling to fasten his anorak while they made their way down the drive. "They didn't even offer us a cup of tea." He gave a satisfied smirk. "But I reckon I hit a raw nerve there."

"I don't know about that," Lucy said, worried. "We could be in trouble if he does make an official complaint."

"He won't," her companion said confidently. "He'll be wanting to keep a low profile."

"Mmm . . . maybe. I don't know." She brightened. "But at least I had more success and got Mrs Commandant to open up. Very forthcoming she was."

He glanced sharply at her. "Really? What did she tell you?"

"Everything I wanted to know." She tapped her nose. "You'll find out at the six o'clock conference."

"Be like that then!" Tony said sourly. Then, as they reached their cars, "I'll race you back. It'll give you plenty of time to write your report."

"I'm not racing anywhere in these conditions," Lucy stated.

CHAPTER EIGHTEEN

JULIE PEERED into the bathroom mirror, studying her red, puffy eyes and tear-stained cheeks. She shook her limp bedraggled hair.

"What a bloody mess," she muttered. She turned on the shower and attempted to wash away some of the misery of the previous night. As the warm water did its work, she even managed a small smile, remembering the eight thirty phone call that had roused her.

"Mum!" Richard had sounded anxious. "Has Dad said anything?"

"About what?"

"About me. I think I might have upset him again. He called me last night."

"Oh, yes. He said he was going to have a word with you."

"Yeah, well, he did. I'd had a few drinks, you see. And I, er, told him to piss off. Did he tell you that?"

"No, love, he didn't. We're not exactly on speaking terms at the moment."

"Oh. Right." He paused. "Look, Mum, I've decided to come home."

He'd hung up. After staring at the phone for a few moments, Julie had staggered into the bathroom to be confronted by the mirror's harsh judgement. Richard mustn't see her like this.

Hastily, she dried herself off, dressed and got to work with her make-up. But her hair remained stubbornly unco-operative, forcing her to make a despairing call to Janet, her hairdresser.

"I'm so sorry, Julie, but I'm fully booked," Janet said. "There's no way I can squeeze you in." Then, in response to further pleas, added doubtfully, "Well, the only thing I can suggest . . . I've got a new girl, started yesterday." She lowered her voice. "Seems all right, she had good references. I'll get her to fit you in at around ten, if you can get here by then."

"Thanks, Jan, you're an angel." Julie glanced at the clock. "Better get my skates on."

* * *

She made it to the hairdressers with two minutes to spare and Janet began the introductions.

"Mrs Blade, this is—"

"Becky!" Julie cried.

"Julie!" Becky Hyde smiled broadly.

"Oh. You two know each other then."

"Mr Blade is my husband's boss," Becky said, ushering her new client towards a chair. "Come on, Julie, let's get started. I'm sorry, but I'm a bit pushed for time."

After briefly discussing what should be done with Julie's hair, she switched to the other talent hairdressers have in abundance — gossip.

"That was funny the other night, wasn't it, the way us girls set up my John — the ghosts in the mansion, and the perfume and all that." She chuckled. "You should've seen his face when I finally let on that he'd been had! That Dorothy, she's nice, isn't she? Must be clever to get to detective inspector so young."

Julie's lips tightened but she made no comment. Becky burbled on. "John loves working with Detective

Superintendent Blade. Only the other night he was saying that the boss gives him lots of important jobs. One day he was even left in charge. So your husband must be pleased with him."

She stopped snipping for a moment, waiting for Julie to say something. But Julie made no comment. "The murder case they're investigating is exciting, isn't it? I couldn't believe it when John told me who the suspects—"

Aghast, Julie waved her to silence. "He shouldn't have told you anything. They never talk about cases to anybody outside the force, and you shouldn't ever repeat things you hear." She looked at Becky in the mirror and whispered fiercely, "You never know who might be listening."

Becky almost lost her grip on the scissors. She shot a worried look at her employer, who was busy with another customer and had her back turned.

"Sorry! I won't do it again. Please don't tell Mr Blade. I don't want to get John into trouble."

Julie said nothing. Then, suddenly, the tension gripping her body ebbed away and she relented. "All right. I won't tell Mr Blade." *I'm not talking to the bastard anyway*, she added to herself. "Just warn that young husband of yours to be careful what he talks about in future."

The salon doorbell tinkled. Becky left Julie and hurried over to greet the woman who had entered.

"That's my next client," she said on her return. After that, conversation languished while she hastened to finish doing Julie's hair.

On the way home, Julie decided to cook one of Richard's favourite meals and called into the local supermarket to buy the ingredients. It was an odd choice for such a young man, she was to reflect later as she fried the liver and bacon and made the onion gravy.

With a sigh of satisfaction, Richard pushed his empty plate away. He took a deep breath. "Mum, I had to come home and get things straight with Dad. It's no good trying to do that over the phone. I've been thinking a lot about that

153

woman — the detective inspector he sent to interview me. What she said really annoyed me."

"And me too! I let your father know in no uncertain—"

Richard held up a hand, cutting her short. "No, no, you don't understand what I mean. Her questions upset me at the time, but to be honest, I was quite rude. I reckon *I* probably annoyed *her*. Then last night, when I thought about everything she'd said, I had the feeling that she'd really been trying to help me — you know, get my alibi straight and all that. Anyway, I thought I'd blown it, so I started drinking — and then, when Dad rang, I told him to piss off."

"You can explain it all when he gets in, dear. I'm sure it'll be all right."

Julie felt a pang of guilt, recalling that Blade had also suggested that Dorothy Fraser had been trying to help their son. What if Ralph and Richard were right and she was wrong? Had she been unjust, jumped to hasty conclusions? Guilt and doubt chased each other around her mind. She just didn't know what to think anymore.

She found another reason for remorse. Blade, too, was fond of liver and bacon but she had only bought enough for one. Should she go out into the cold to buy more? Was she being too hard on him? No, she decided. The bastard had acted insufferably. It would just have to be a bloody cheese omelette. She thought again. Well, maybe she could give him an extra helping of chips.

CHAPTER NINETEEN

AS SOON as the door closed behind Dorothy, Blade leaned forward, elbows on the desk, his head in his hands. The day had hardly begun but already he felt exhausted, his mind dull. With his team absent, gone about their assigned tasks, the silence was somehow menacing. He had never felt so alone.

He recalled Stan Oliver's earlier phone call. Not only was he on the verge of losing the chief constable's support but his son had sworn at him and it seemed that his wife's love for him had turned into — surely not — *hate*.

He sat up straight, knuckling his eyes and forcing himself to concentrate on the double murder investigation. He had a full programme planned for the day but he was running out of time. He had to act.

Pulling out his mobile, Blade made an appointment to see a judge with whom he'd had dealings in the past. Then he left his office and went to the incident room to study the pictures on the board and focus his ideas.

Dorothy was standing there, doing that very thing.

"What are you doing here? I thought you'd gone to London ages ago," he grumbled.

"Well, I was just—"

Felicity Dumble walked in. "I was passing the end of the corridor and saw you come in here," she said to Blade, giving Dorothy a friendly smile. "How's the case going?"

"Very well," he answered easily, with what he hoped was an impish grin. He nodded towards the board. "It was one of them who dunnit."

"Hmm . . ." Lips pursed, she leant forward to get a closer look. "I heard that you'd stuck our picture up. I can't say I approve of that, Superintendent, because," she forced a smile, "if I'd known it was going to finish up on display I'd have worn something more glamorous."

"You got it the wrong way around, it's *you* who can make any clothes look glamorous . . . ma'am."

She coloured. "Oh, um, well, I'm glad everything's going all right. Must be off, things to do. The chief is away again today, he's been called back to the Home Office." She lowered her voice to a loud whisper and glanced around furtively. "I think it will be good news, so he'll be in a happy mood when he gets back."

She turned on her heel and was gone.

"Well, I'm glad she told us," Dorothy said. "I don't think I should go to London now, so I'll get my Bob to see if his contact can find out what's going on. It would be embarrassing if I got caught by our great Mr Chaytor-Gill," she hesitated, "*nosing about* at the Home Office."

Blade grinned. "Yeah, you're right. And I'm glad I found you before you left, because I've got another job for you."

Indicating for her to follow, he led the way back to his office. Dorothy sat down on the opposite side of his desk. Blade stroked his jaw, appearing to stare straight through her, silent. She began to shift about uncomfortably. Then, suddenly, he came to a decision, speaking rapidly.

"We've got to wrap this up, Dorothy. Today! That call I took this morning was to tell me that the chief constable is under pressure to hand the case over to the Yard. But I think you and I are both working along the same lines and, together, we can crack it before that happens."

Taking her fully into his confidence, Blade went on to explain his theories while she nodded enthusiastically and with growing excitement. His suspicions exactly mirrored her own.

"We must cover every angle, rule out any false leads and find the proof. I've been personally investigating the death of the security chap, Roger Cotter. I was going to see his widow again today, because I have some more questions for her about possible suspects, especially now that our own pathologist has entered the frame. What connection could Dr Stoker have with Mr Cotter? Is there a connection serious enough to drive him to commit murder? But I'll trust you to find the answers to those questions . . . now you're at a loose end." He raised a tired smile at her look of indignation. "I'm running out of time, you see, so you can go and see Mrs Cotter."

* * *

When Dorothy had departed, Blade called Headley on his mobile.

"Where are you, Bill?"

"Bramshill, sir, with the security men."

"Good. Drop what you're doing and get across here now. My office. I've got a new task for you, and it's urgent."

When his trusted veteran detective constable arrived, Blade nodded towards the chair just vacated by Dorothy.

"Sit down, Bill, and take notes of everything I want you to do. I'm having to push everything forward or we won't have a case to investigate because it will go to the Met. I've trawled through all the evidence gathered by you and the rest of the team — as you know, they're still out there now, collecting more facts — and I feel sure I know who is responsible for both murders. So, I want you to spend the rest of today organising an operation for tomorrow. It's going to be make-or-break day."

Blade went on to explain his theories and detail Bill Headley's own part in the plan of action, finishing with,

"It's going to be a matter of timing. You know the experts you'll need to recruit. It will be up to you to have them on standby, ready to act the moment you get the signal from me. Impress on them that speed is vital — and you must ring me the moment you get the data, so don't forget to make sure your mobile is fully charged. You'll need help tomorrow," he added as an afterthought, "so you can have Tony. I'll brief him after this evening's conference."

When Headley had gone, Blade checked his watch, noting in surprise that it was only 10.47 a.m. He knuckled his tired eyes, feeling as though he'd already done a day's work. There was still more than an hour to go before he needed to leave for his appointment. He tried to keep focused on the job in hand — deciding how to convince the judge to grant him a search warrant.

But his thoughts kept wandering to Julie and what had been said the night before. Should he ring her? Try to smooth things over? No. But even as he reached that decision, his finger was pressing the number. He heard his own voice telling him that his call could not be taken at the moment but if he left his name and number . . .

He cut the connection angrily. He guessed she'd recognised his mobile number and just wasn't bloody picking up. Should he try her mobile? No. The result would be the same. Meanwhile, at that very moment, unbeknownst to him, Julie was entering her hairdresser's salon.

Perhaps a visit to the first crime scene — the chest that had held Harold Ashington's body — might get his mind back on track. Slamming his office door behind him, he left the building. As soon as he stepped outside, he was buffeted by a blast of biting arctic wind that made him gasp as if someone had thrown a bucket of icy water over him. Hail lashing his face, he ran across the deserted campus and hurried up the steps of the mansion and into the warmth. Inside, he closed the magnificent oak portal and leaned back against it, breathing fast.

All was silent. The lights were low, the hall deserted. The chest was still in place, the lid open as usual.

He took a pace towards it then stopped at the sound of a woman's voice.

"*You don't really think he'll take you with him, do you? Believe me, he'll leave you behind,*" a contemptuous laugh, "*and you'll become just one more Bramshill ghost.*"

Blade looked around. The hall was empty. Recalling the story of John Hyde's spectral experience, he smiled faintly. He knew where Dorothy was, so they weren't doing the same to him. He reminded himself that he didn't believe in ghosts.

And anyway, he'd recognised the voice.

He changed direction and headed for the commandant's office whose outer door was ajar. He pushed it wide. Felicity, who was standing near the desk, turned to face him. Her face, already flushed with anger, turned an even deeper red.

"Oh!"

"We meet again." Blade greeted her cheerfully, giving no indication of having overheard her outburst. He inclined his head towards the woman seated at the desk, his eyebrows raised in inquiry.

"Er, this is Helena Willerby, Mr Chaytor-Gill's secretary," Felicity said.

"Ah, the very lady we need to see. Are you feeling better now? I heard you'd been ill. I was going to disturb your peace later today and send one of my people to see you. I'm Detective Superintendent Blade, by the way. But now, here you are and here am I, so it might as well be me. Do you mind if I sit?"

Without waiting for a reply, he sat down facing the secretary across the desk. "Nothing to worry about," he said. "Just some questions. You might be able to help us clear up a few points . . ."

He paused, glancing up at Felicity, who stood for a few seconds looking flustered. Then she went to the door. "I'll leave you to it. Things to do." It seemed to be her stock phrase.

Blade turned to face Helena Willerby, who was regarding him with amusement. She showed no sign of nervousness.

But that wasn't the only surprising thing about her. In her late thirties, she was much younger than he'd expected. Shoulder-length ginger hair, layered so as to frame the shape of her face and its high cheekbones, emphasised large, sparkling grey-green eyes. Her full lips were slightly parted to reveal even, white teeth. Unlike Sylvia Ashington, there was not a freckle in sight, just a birthmark in the centre of her left cheek. Her jawline, while hinting at strength of character, made her chin stick out just a little too much. Although she was seated — straight-backed, with one arm resting casually on the desktop — Blade guessed that she was tall . . . and noted that her warm, white sweater did nothing to disguise the fact that she was quite big-framed.

The detective's sharp eyes took in all these things, as well as the black anorak hanging by its hood on the clothes stand. He opened his mouth to speak, then closed it again, a sudden thought flashing into his head:

Hooded, in a poor light, she could be taken for a man.

He pushed the idea to the back of his mind for now and had another go. "I must say, you look very fit for someone recovering from flu."

"Oh, it wasn't flu, just a cold. I throw that sort of thing off easily because, yes, I *am* very fit. I work hard at it. I run, play squash and hockey." She chuckled. "Plus, of course, I made sure I had plenty of hot whisky to wash down the paracetamol."

All at once her amused expression was gone. "You'll have gathered that the high-flying Felicity Dumble and I don't get on. Did you hear what she was saying just before you came in?"

"Something about you being a Bramshill ghost?" He gave a slight smile.

"Yes, of course you heard, and you're wondering what it was all about. Well, I'll tell you. She came here to gloat about Roderick's new job — Chief Inspector of Constabulary, confirmed this morning. Did you know about that?" He nodded. "She said Rod would soon be gone, and that he'd be glad to see the back of me. According to Felicity, he was going to try to get her in as an inspector."

Helena paused for breath. "That's when I got mad. I said that I already knew he had the job because he'd rung to tell me. I couldn't resist adding that, far from leaving me behind, he'd even fixed it for me to go with him, because the in-post secretary intends to retire when the present CIoC quits. It's all part of the deal." Blade raised his eyebrows. "It's true. And that's what the argument was about."

"Hmm . . . your boss seems very keen to keep you. He must be happy with your work," Blade said.

"Rod and I go back years. I used to do a lot of work for him at Scotland Yard, when he was a commander and I was in the typing pool. Soon after he got the top job here, at Bramshill, the secretary who was here decided to leave — I don't think they got on — and that's when he persuaded me to join him."

"And you've lived happily ever after."

Helena frowned. "It was fine at first, until *she* arrived to serve as his deputy after losing her job as a chief constable. She set her cap at him right from the start."

"You mean they had an affair?"

"Well, what do you think? She's a bloody good looker. And clever with it. Of course, they . . ." She stopped speaking for a moment. "They could have — but I doubt it. Any scandal would end Mr Chaytor-Gill's chances of an inspectorate."

"The affair could have started before the IOC vacancy came up for grabs," Blade suggested, adding casually, "And what about you? Are *you* having an affair with your boss? Could that be the real cause of the enmity between you and Mrs Dumble?"

"How dare you," Helena snapped, flushing. "That's downright rude. You have no right to make such insinuations. You come in here—"

Blade raised his hand. He nodded towards her own hand, lying flat on the desktop as if it had nothing to do with her. She appeared rather ineffectually, to be concealing a book.

"And what are you trying to hide there?" he asked. "It wouldn't happen to be the office diary, would it? We've been looking for that. Where was it? It wasn't in your desk drawer."

He leaned across to pull the diary towards him and she snatched her hand away. Suddenly she seemed wary. "It was in the filing cabinet. I always lock it in there when I leave at night. I suppose I must have done that automatically when I went home early."

Blade was busy leafing through the diary, searching for the date.

"Here we are," he said. "The twenty-second of February, the day Harold Ashington was murdered . . ." He stiffened, adding slowly, "and the day he was due to see the commandant at one fifteen p.m."

He looked across at her, waiting for her response.

"The appointment was cancelled," Helena said quickly. "As you see, it's been crossed out."

"Yes, I do see." He looked pointedly at the pen on the otherwise empty desktop. "I'm also wondering *when* it was crossed out. It's strange, isn't it, that the commandant hasn't ever mentioned having an appointment with Mr Ashington at around the time of his death."

"That's because he never knew." Helena had recovered her poise and looked him straight in the eye. "Rod, er, Mr Chaytor-Gill, didn't know about the appointment. I never mentioned it to him. There was no need. Mr Ashington came into this office, booked the meeting, then an hour or so later came back and cancelled it, saying he'd dealt with the matter. I crossed it out then."

Blade glanced at his watch. It was time to go. He mustn't keep the judge waiting.

He stood up. "That's all for now, Miss Willerby, but I shall need to speak to you again."

"Just tell me when, Superintendent," she said coolly, "and I'll arrange for my solicitor to be present. I'm not at all happy with the way you have spoken to me, probing my

162

private life and making suggestions. Are you allowed to do that? I found it most offensive. Shouldn't you have cautioned me or something?"

He stared at her for a few seconds, then, with a curt, "I'll be in touch," turned on his heel and left.

Outside, the hail had stopped, but the biting east wind still snatched his breath away. He ran back to his office to collect his anorak. On the way out again, he decided to call into the incident room to see if there were any messages for him. The sight of a familiar figure brought him up short.

"What the hell are you doing here?"

Adrian Harper grinned. "I went to see the doc, sir, and he said I was fit for light duties." He reached into his pocket and pulled out a piece of paper. "Here! I've got a certificate." He proceeded to tell Blade of Angela Liddell's progress, omitting to reveal that this visit had taken place *before* he had the certificate.

"Good," said Blade. "Now I want you to start putting together a full report on Miss Helena Willerby, the commandant's secretary — family background, education, career and anything else you can dig up. But be discreet, don't let her get any hint of what you're doing. She's back in her office today, so be careful. If Lucy comes back early from her interview, get her to help you."

He glanced again at his watch. Three minutes past twelve. Dammit.

"Must dash. Important meeting," he called over his shoulder as he hurried out to his car.

He knew it would take about forty-five minutes to get to Winchester on the M3. The judge, who was presiding over a case at the Crown Court, had agreed to see him at his lodgings during the lunch recess at one o'clock.

* * *

The judge listened attentively, while devouring a dish of succulent roast beef with all the trimmings, followed by a very tasty looking apple crumble and custard. Then, as he stirred his coffee, he looked across the table at his visitor who, he declared, had made a fair case. Blade got his search warrant — but no lunch.

Now, back on the M3, he was hungry. He decided to stop at Basingstoke, where he bought a soggy sandwich and coffee and, thus refreshed, visited Chief Superintendent Stan Oliver at police HQ.

"Things are hotting up, sir, so I thought it would be better to see you in person rather than rely on a hasty phone call," he began. "I have a lot to tell you — and a lot to ask."

"Ask away, Ralph."

"Can I move out of Bramshill and bring the team back here? Tomorrow?"

"No problem. Your space is still here. What's the rush?"

"A witness — a possible suspect — worried me a bit this morning. She challenged my right to question her and spoke about a solicitor. She's worked a lot with the police, and so she's familiar with procedure—"

"Ah! Shades of Code C of the Police and Criminal Procedure Act," Oliver interjected. "You're thinking about Detective Superintendent Steve Fulcher, who lost his job after he breached it."

Blade nodded. "That's exactly what's on my mind."

"If I remember correctly," Oliver said, "the serial killer, Christopher Halliwell, was arrested in a car park where he was cautioned and formally charged with kidnapping a missing woman. Halliwell should then have been taken to a police station, cautioned again and told he had a right to a solicitor. But that didn't happen, because after the arrest, during a long chat with DS Fulcher, Halliwell confessed to not only the murder of the missing woman, but also another one, and offered to show Fulcher the field where he'd hidden the bodies."

Blade nodded again. "That's right. They drove straight there, instead of going to the police station. I daresay DS Fulcher was scared Halliwell might change his mind. But

Code C had been infringed and, as result of that, some of his evidence was ruled inadmissible in court. And that's what is worrying me, sir. When this case eventually comes to trial, I don't want to lose it through having bent the rules. I want to make sure everything is watertight and straightforward. But you told me this morning that time is running out and the chief constable is under mounting pressure," He drew in a deep breath, "so I've decided to speed things up."

Blade went on to bring his boss up to date, finishing with the events of that morning — his encounter with Helena Willerby and the procurement of the search warrant.

"Please would you try to persuade the chief constable to come to Bramshill at ten o'clock tomorrow morning? By then, I shall be ready to give him the whole story and put this case to bed. But don't let on that you already know my plans. You could suggest that, as I'm pulling out of the college, it might be a nice gesture if he were to take the opportunity to thank the commandant for his help and hospitality. That would give him a good excuse to pay a visit."

"Don't worry. If he thinks you're going to wrap the case up, wild horses won't keep him away," Oliver assured him.

* * *

When Blade came out of his office at six o'clock, the team were all in place around the table, ready to give their reports.

He turned to Adrian first. "Helena Willerby, the commandant's secretary. What can you tell us about her?"

"Not a lot, sir. We haven't had much time. Lucy helped me after she'd done her report on her own inquiry but it's a bit awkward asking questions without her getting wind of it, with her being on the premises. Anyway, she's forty-one years old, public school education, degree in ancient history from Birmingham University, brought up in Surrey to wealthy parents — father an accountant with his own business — and she owns her own house down the road in Hartley Wintney, probably thanks to Dad. Before coming here as Mr Chaytor-Gill's secretary — she says 'PA', it sounds posher I suppose — she worked at Scotland Yard, where she was well thought of."

Next, Tony Robinson and Lucy recounted their interviews with Mr Dumble and Mrs Chaytor-Gill. Blade listened carefully, occasionally jotting down notes or asking a question.

Then it was Dorothy's turn. She reported finding Mrs Cotter still grieving over the loss of her husband, and full of praise for the commandant. "'They were friends, you know, my Roger and Mr Chaytor-Gill,'" she told me. 'Such a lovely man. They became close when my husband was changing all the security stuff at Bramshill —Rog and Rod he used to say.' Mrs Cotter told me the commandant had been to see her the day after Roger's murder to offer his condolences. Apparently, he was very concerned for her welfare. He asked if she needed money or other help — she didn't — and promised to see that she was treated fairly over pensions and so on. She kept repeating that he was 'such a lovely man.' But that wasn't the only surprise." Dorothy looked across at Blade. "That came when I got to the other question you wanted answered. Yes, Mr Cotter *did* know Dr Stoker. Mrs Cotter had no doubt about that. She recalled her husband telling her that in the course of checking the security at Bramshill's laboratory, he'd had an interesting chat with the pathologist — she even remembered the name Stoker. Not only that, the doctor had told him about a lecture he'd given to senior policemen earlier that afternoon. Apparently Mr Cotter was so impressed with it that he repeated the gist of it to his wife. And the subject?" Dorothy paused for dramatic effect. "Cyanide! It seems that Dr Stoker had revealed several interesting facts about the poison — and had even taken a bottle out of a cabinet so that Mr Cotter could smell it."

There was an immediate buzz of excitement and the detectives all started talking among themselves, until the inspector called for silence.

"But, sir," she said to Blade, "I also — as you asked — had another think about the morning of Mr Cotter's murder, from the moment he arrived at his office until the moment he was found dead." Reading from her notes, she went on, "Mr Cotter arrived for work as usual at seven thirty a.m. but left his office almost immediately, after receiving a phone call. At about seven fifty, Angela Liddell came into the ops room to report finding Mr Cotter's body in her room. You and Sergeant Hyde ran across to check, but you didn't go inside the room. You came back, leaving John on guard to make sure no one crossed the threshold, and at seven fifty-six precisely — I checked the time — you rang Dr Stoker at his home. He arrived, and was logged in at the gate, at five past eight."

She drew in a deep breath. "So, I really don't see how it could be possible for Dr Stoker to have killed Mr Cotter, say sometime between seven thirty and seven fifty, and been home in time to answer our callout on his landline phone — all without anyone, including the people on the gate, noticing his earlier presence here. The journey from his house takes at least fifty minutes, even with a clear road and no hold-ups."

"Mmm, that's a good point," Blade said thoughtfully. "Maybe Fred Stoker didn't do the deed himself, but it adds credibility to our theory that there are *two* people involved in these murders. And we have established that there is a link between our Fred and the second victim, Mr Cotter."

Lucy put her hand up. "And between Dr Stoker and the first victim, Harold Ashington, sir."

Blade stared at her. "How do you mean?"

"When the investigation started, sir, you gave Constable Harper and me the task of interviewing all the students in Syndicate Six to check if any of them had some sort of connection to Mr Ashington. Well, when Inspector Fraser spoke just now about the doctor's lecture on cyanide, it jogged my memory. Mrs Felicity Dumble, who's in charge of Syndicate Six, mentioned that lecture, and I remember her telling me that Mr Ashington had seemed very interested in it, and afterwards had had quite a long, animated conversation with Dr Stoker."

"Why didn't you report this before?" Blade asked sharply.

Lucy blinked. "Because at that time there was no suggestion that Dr Stoker was involved. He was the pathologist, not a suspect. Anyway, you told me to check on the victim's fellow students," she answered defensively.

John Hyde came to her rescue. "She's right, sir. None of us has had any reason to doubt Dr Stoker until now. But if the things I was told in London today are true—"

Blade swung round to face him. "Aha! Come on, John. What have you got?"

"I'll keep it short, but what I've got is the reason why Dr Stoker moved to this area," Hyde began. "According to the gossip in the Yard, Ashington and Stoker have history. Apart from occasionally working together, they also began to meet socially because they lived fairly close to each other in north London. Too close, as it turned out, because the wives became involved as well — meals out, visits to each other's homes, that sort of thing. That's how Ashington met the doctor's daughter, who was seventeen at the time, and being the nasty bastard that he was, he seduced her. There were rows, but Ashington continued to see her, treating Dr Stoker's protests with contempt. Even worse, the daughter became besotted with him."

"In the end, the doc and his wife decided that the only thing to do was move away. So, they came here. I'm told it seems to have worked, because the daughter did well at school and went on to university. She's now in her late twenties — and still single."

There was a heavy silence. Eventually, Blade said, "And then, after all that time, poor Fred Stoker comes face to face with his old adversary while he happens to be giving a lecture. On cyanide."

John Hyde spoke quickly. "Hang on, sir. I don't think we should jump to conclusions. Before I left for London this morning, I called into the lab. That bottle of cyanide you asked me to get tested was full and hadn't been interfered with."

"It still sounds like a good motive for murder," Tony Robinson said. "He must have thought the whole thing was going to start again."

Blade shook his head. "No, I think our sergeant is right, and we mustn't jump to conclusions. That was good work, John, and you too, Dorothy." He nodded to each of them, before turning to the team at large. "If you've been gossiping to the civilian staff — who're already getting their stuff together — you've probably heard that we're moving out of here tomorrow. But that's not all." He paused dramatically.

"We're going out with a bang. I'm calling it 'Operation Bramshill'."

He went on to detail the part each member of the team was to play in the planned operation, concentrating on the roles of Bill Headley and Tony Robinson. He sent the team home at seven o'clock, but the day wasn't over for him. He went to his office and sat at his desk, worrying. Was he right? His gut told him he was, but could he prove it? That would depend on how things went tomorrow. He went over the plan yet again.

* * *

After another very long day, Blade finally got home at about nine. As he stepped into the hall, he could hear the TV in the sitting room and was tempted to creep past and go straight up to bed. He had never felt so drained, and the sick, hollow feeling in the pit of his stomach wasn't just hunger. The thought of another row with Julie filled him with dread. Tentatively, he opened the door.

"At last! You're back!" Julie jumped up from her chair. She looked — could it be? — pleased to see him.

"Dad!" Richard, who had been lying on the settee, scrambled to his feet and hurried across to hug his father. A welter of questions and answers flew across the room.

"Have you had anything to eat?"

"What are you doing here?"

"I had a sandwich."

"I came to see you . . . to say sorry."

"I'll go and do your meal."

"I must get to bed."

Julie was hurrying to the kitchen, so she didn't hear that last comment. Richard switched the TV off before dragging him across to the settee.

"You'll love the dinner, Dad. It's liver and bacon."

A tiny, hesitant smile flickered at the corners of Blade's mouth before the warmth of the fire and the soft sofa lulled him to sleep.

Twenty minutes later, he was woken by Richard and his mother, who steered him into the dining room and sat him at the table.

Bleary-eyed, he stared down at the omelette — with its large helping of chips — then up at his son.

"Sorry," said Richard. "I thought it was the same as what I had — liver and bacon."

"I'll do that for you tomorrow," Julie promised, looking contrite.

"Bed," Blade murmured.

They helped him upstairs.

CHAPTER TWENTY

A REFRESHED Blade parked in front of the mansion just before nine the next morning. Still trying to make it up to him, Julie had risen early, and by the time he was dressed, she had his usual cereal and orange juice ready on the table, followed by fried egg, bacon, mushrooms, sausage and fried tomatoes, with toast and marmalade to finish.

As he got out of his car, Felicity and Chaytor-Gill, who were standing and talking at the foot of Bramshill's front steps, waved to him and came across.

"I hear you're leaving us, Superintendent," said the commandant.

"That's right. Good morning, sir, ma'am." Felicity acknowledged the greeting with a smile. "It's time for us to go home. It's been most helpful, being able to work 'on-the-spot', as it were, and I'm very grateful for your hospitality. But, well, you know, official procedures, interviews recorded under proper conditions and all that. Everything by the book . . ." He trailed off.

Chaytor-Gill laughed. "Well, we should know, we teach it! But I'm surprised. Are you that far advanced already?"

Like a bad stage actor, Blade looked around furtively. He leaned towards them and lowered his voice. "I'm hoping to make arrests today."

Felicity and Chaytor-Gill glanced at each other.

"Seriously?" Felicity said.

"May I ask who . . . ?"

"I couldn't possibly tell you at this stage," Blade said. "Even my own chief constable doesn't know yet. I haven't had a chance to—"

"Ah, your chief constable," the commandant broke in. "Funny you should mention Bainbridge. He rang me last night to say he was coming here and asked if he could pop in to see me. Something about wanting to thank me personally. He said he'd be with me sometime before ten."

"That makes sense, he's, er, killing two birds with one stone, you might say. He's due to meet me at ten, when I'll be giving him a full briefing on the progress in the case — and reporting on the arrests." Blade looked at his watch. "So, I'd better get my skates on and get ready for him."

He spun on his heel and walked away, calling back over his shoulder, "If you ask him nicely, he might let you sit in. You'll have all the answers then."

* * *

Chief Constable Clive Bainbridge was late, finally marching into the conference room with Chief Superintendent Stan Oliver at ten fifteen. They were accompanied by the commandant and Felicity.

"I hope you don't mind, Superintendent. Mr Chaytor-Gill and Mrs Dumble asked if they could sit in."

His tone made it clear that they'd be sitting in whether he minded or not. Bainbridge was accustomed to getting his own way. Although of average height, he was heavily built, with the muscles of a weightlifter and tree-trunk legs. For all his bulk, there wasn't an ounce of fat on him. In days gone by, fleeing wrongdoers had discovered that trying to get past him was like running into a brick wall. Now, at fifty-four, his hair was greying, as were the bushy eyebrows that almost hid a pair of deep-set brown eyes. A broad, flat nose above a slightly jutting bottom lip and a strong jaw added to his somewhat belligerent look.

"Of course. They're very welcome," Blade assured him, smiling at the new arrivals. "It may be a bit of a squash in the office, so perhaps we should stay out here." He turned to address Hyde. "Sergeant, will you bring those chairs back, please? We can all sit around the table. Oh, and bring the photo board out as well."

With much scraping of chairs, the company sat themselves down. Blade was seated at the end of the table nearest to his office, with the chief constable at the other end. On the chief's right sat Stan Oliver. John Hyde was midway down the table, the board, propped on its easel, beside him. He was holding a pointer. Dorothy sat on the opposite side of the table, close to Blade, with Felicity and Chaytor-Gill between her and the chief constable.

Once everyone was settled, Blade began. "As this is our last day at Bramshill, I thought it appropriate to invite the chief constable here so that we could brief him on the progress we've made in the investigation into the murders of Chief Superintendent Harold Ashington, who was on a senior command course, and Mr Roger Cotter, the college security manager." He paused. "Today is also the day when," he glanced at his watch, "just over half an hour ago, Operation Bramshill was launched." Another pause. "An operation that I hope will *by the time this meeting ends*, put me in a position to make arrests. This briefing will fill in—"

"Just a moment, Superintendent," Chief Constable Bainbridge roared, looking around the table. "I don't see anyone taking notes. I want a full transcript of this meeting in case I need to refer to it later."

Blade was nonplussed. "Oh, I, er, we don't have a shorthand—"

"What about that lot next door?" the chief demanded.

"No, I don't think they—"

Dorothy looked at Chaytor-Gill. "Your secretary came back yesterday, sir, surely she . . ."

"Get her!" Bainbridge boomed. Then, as the commandant struggled to get up, added, "Don't waste time, man, ring her."

Obediently, Chaytor-Gill pulled out his mobile and, while everyone listened, instructed Helena Willerby to join them immediately, bringing her shorthand notebook.

Four minutes later there was a knock, and the door was opened by a uniformed constable who called, "Lady says she was told to come here."

Blade nodded and beckoned to an apprehensive-looking Helena. A number of other uniformed police were visible, standing around not far from the door. Ignoring the detective's summons, Helena made straight for her boss, who shook his head and waved her towards Blade, who then explained her duties. There were two empty chairs between him and John Hyde. Helena chose the one next to the sergeant.

While her hand glided over the pages of her notebook, Blade resumed his briefing. He began with 'the usual suspects' — the wife and her lover — while Sergeant Hyde used his pointer to tap the pictures of Sylvia Ashington and Jack Wriggley.

Just as he began to summarise his and Dorothy's interviews, there was yet another interruption. They heard scuffling in the corridor, and someone shouting, "Let me in! I know where his office is. I want to see him. Now!"

The door opened and the same PC said, "I'm sorry, sir, there's—"

"Let him in," Blade said.

The constable moved aside and the man, still shouting angrily, was abruptly released by the two policemen who had been holding him back. He pitched forward and almost fell into the conference room. Only after regaining his balance did he seem to become aware of all the people seated around the table, staring at him.

His eyes on the chief constable's impressive uniform epaulettes, he looked embarrassed. "Oh."

Blade stood up. "Come and sit next to me, Fred," he said, indicating the empty chair.

In a flash, the fury was back, and his face turned brick red.

"I want to see you . . ." He spotted Hyde on the other side of the table. "And you, Sergeant bloody Hyde. How dare you go around trying to fit me up with your damned murders. I've got friends, you know. I've heard all about you sniffing around the Yard yesterday, asking questions about me. And getting my cyanide analysed at the lab — not *my* lab, of course. And *you*," he turned on Dorothy, "quizzing Mrs Cotter about me and her husband. I rang her last night, and she told me about your visit. Oh yes, I've got friends."

Chief Constable Bainbridge stood up. He spoke mildly, his voice bearing no trace of its usual hectoring tone. "Dr Stoker, we've never met but I know who you are, and I'm familiar with all the good work you've done for us. Now, why don't you sit down, as Superintendent Blade suggests? He might have something of interest to say to you."

Blade shot his boss a bemused glance, unused to seeing this gentle side of him.

After some initial hesitation, Stoker moved across to the empty chair between Blade and Helena, who gave him a faint smile, which he returned with one of his own.

"Of course," Blade said, noticing this exchange, "You two are old friends. I was forgetting. You worked together at the Yard years ago, and now here you are, together again at Bramshill. But let's get on . . ."

"Yes, let's," Bainbridge growled, his tone truculent again. "We've had enough interruptions."

Still standing, Blade continued, Hyde's pointer working overtime as the various people in the photographs were discussed — and then dismissed.

"It soon became obvious to us that whoever committed the murders would have to know Bramshill intimately, both the workings of the college and its geography. And there would have to be *two* killers. It would have been physically impossible for one person to carry out the murders. So, we had to find people with a common motive, and either prove their guilt or clear them. But to prove guilt we needed one vital thing — evidence."

Blade looked down at Stoker. "That was part of yesterday's exercise, Fred. You and your friend, Miss Willerby, were in the frame because you each had both the motive and an intimate knowledge of Bramshill, including . . ."

Helena's pen slid across the paper, leaving a heavy trail of black ink. Stoker sat, frozen.

The notes of *Für Elise* filled the silence.

Blade pulled out his mobile, listened, and said, "Right. I'll come out." He pocketed the phone and hurried to the door, calling, "I'll be back in five minutes."

The chief constable muttered a curse.

* * *

Blade found Bill Headley and Tony Robinson waiting for him, just far enough down the corridor to be out of view through the long window.

Outside the incident room all was quiet. The civilian staff, accompanied by Adrian and Lucy, had left for divisional police headquarters. Apart from the policemen watching the door, Bramshill was empty.

It took less than five minutes for Headley to give Blade the information he needed. He returned to the conference room accompanied by his two detectives and marched back to his place where he remained standing, Bill and Tony behind him.

"Now, where was I?" he resumed, stroking his chin. "Ah, yes. Evidence. As I was saying, Fred . . ." He looked down at Stoker, slumped in his chair, the earlier angry red of his face superseded by an unhealthy pallor. At the sound of his name, he lifted his head slightly, his eyes dull. Beside him, Helena sat straight, stiff, knees together, hands clasping and unclasping.

"Evidence, Fred," Blade continued, "and now I have it. Earlier, I mentioned an 'Operation Bramshill', which — I can tell you now — has been entirely successful. Detective

176

Constables Headley and Robinson will explain all shortly, but first," Blade smiled, anticipating the revelation, "there are two arrests to be made."

He looked towards the door and beckoned. The four uniformed constables entered and stood just inside the room. He then nodded at Dorothy and Hyde, who both stood up and moved quickly to stand by the suspects.

Dorothy spoke first. "Roderick Chaytor-Gill, you are under arrest on suspicion of the murder of Harold Ashington. You do not have to say anything, but it may harm your defence if you do not mention when questioned something which you later rely on in court. Anything you do say may be given in evidence."

The commandant, purple with anger, was on his feet and about to speak, but Felicity was quicker. She dodged past Hyde and placed a restraining hand on Chaytor-Gill's sleeve. "Don't say anything," she hissed, before Hyde caught up with her to arrest her in turn, charging her with the murder of Roger Cotter.

Dorothy then ordered the commandant to hand over his mobile phone, which he did with ill grace. She passed it to Bill Headley, who was waiting nearby. He almost ran back to the table with it.

Blade signalled to the policemen, who handcuffed the prisoners and led them away to two waiting police cars. They would be kept apart from now on. While Chaytor-Gill protested furiously, Felicity remained silent and calm. As she turned to go, Felicity gave Blade a fleeting smile.

Ignoring her, Blade turned to John and Dorothy. "Off you go. Don't forget, everything by the book. When you get to the police station, charge them again and tell them their rights."

Bill and Tony were huddled together at the table, examining the commandant's mobile. At the other end, Stoker and Helena looked almost fully restored, the threat of imminent arrest having been lifted, but they still seemed nervous. Helena, in particular, lacked her usual self-confidence.

"Sorry I had to put you through that, Fred," Blade began, "but I had to be sure that I was right, which meant I had to prolong things until I got the phone call from Bill Headley. And, you *did* give us grounds for suspicion. You must have recognised Ashington when you saw his body that first night, but you kept quiet about his identity and your link with him."

"That makes two of us," Dr Stoker pointed out.

"Touché," Blade acknowledged with a small smile. "But no harm done. That man is out of your hair now — and mine. I hope you and I can resume our former friendly relationship and continue to work well together. But as for you, Miss Willerby," he said, "you have committed a crime. It was you who crossed out the diary appointment, wasn't it? Ashington never cancelled the meeting. He went — and was killed by Chaytor-Gill. And when you came back to work yesterday, you erased the entry. Why?"

"I was trying to help Rod — er, the commandant. I knew Ashington was blackmailing him—"

"About what?"

"The job. The affair he was having with that woman, Felicity Dumble. If the Home Office heard about it, he wouldn't have got the job. And he was going to take *me* with him, not her. She wasn't good enough for him. But Ashington found out about the affair and—"

Blade stopped her in her tracks. "It wasn't an affair. Even Ashington got that bit wrong. It was a wife swap. When Chaytor-Gill was safely in his new job, he planned to divorce his wife, Anthea, and marry Felicity, after she had divorced her husband, Keith Dumble. Then Anthea would marry Keith."

Helena stared at him. "You're lying," she shouted. "It's me he really loves. You're just trying to make me say things."

Blade shook his head. "No, Miss Willerby, I'm not lying. I suggest you go home now, have a good night's rest and come to the police station tomorrow to make a proper statement under caution." As she left the room, he called after her, "And bring your solicitor with you."

When she'd gone, he sent a much relieved Dr Stoker home. He took the chief constable and Stan Oliver to the canteen, where he'd arranged for them both to have lunch, and where he collected sandwiches and a large flask of tea for his two detective constables and himself.

* * *

After lunch, the two senior officers found Blade in his office, sitting at his desk along with Headley and Robinson. The three of them had been working on a summary of the investigation.

Blade explained. "It was a remark by Detective Inspector Fraser, and I quote, 'I think there's a rabbit away there', that made me wonder about Chaytor-Gill and Mrs Dumble just after our first meeting with them. At that meeting, he happened to be reminded of an appointment at the Home Office. Fraser also heard Chaytor-Gill whisper to Mrs Dumble, 'I will make a lady of you'. In her reply, she called him 'Sir Rod'."

"Naturally, they didn't know the inspector can lip-read. Chaytor-Gill had applied for the post of Inspector of Constabulary and any hint of scandal would have scuppered his chances. Somehow, Ashington had found out about his relationship with Felicity — he had a reputation for uncovering secrets and using that knowledge to his own advantage."

Blade looked at the chief constable. "You heard what his secretary, Miss Willerby, said when we were all in the conference room. She knew that Chaytor-Gill was being blackmailed by Ashington. And blackmail is a strong motive for murder. We'll come back to that later, but let's move on. Who first pointed us in the direction of Inspector Angela Liddell? Mrs Felicity Dumble. She told us that Angela had a relationship with Ashington, they argued, and she stabbed him with a pair of scissors. All true, up to a point, but she'd twisted the facts. Later, when Mr Cotter's body was found in Angela's room and things were looking black for her, who was extraordinarily kind? Mrs Dumble again. She lent Angela a dressing gown, let her use her apartment, and then relocated her nearby. But why was Mr Cotter in Angela's room in the first place? It was suggested that she'd been having an affair with him — poor young woman, reduced to dating middle-aged men. But this didn't explain why he had to die. I decided it had to do with security, Cotter being the expert on the surveillance cameras. It was Cotter who'd installed the system. So, I questioned his staff, and they confirmed that Chaytor-Gill seemed obsessed by the system. He'd been instructed on how to operate it and had often been shown around by the proud manager. And then I recalled that at our first meeting with Chaytor-Gill, I mentioned that I wanted to see Mr Cotter as soon as he arrived the next morning. Which is when Chaytor-Gill decided that poor Cotter had to die before he could point the finger at him. He knew the manager was always there by seven thirty, so he would have to act quickly."

Blade paused again and raised a finger. "But who could *not* possibly have carried out the murder? Mr Chaytor-Gill. There were witnesses galore — including the next prime suspect, Angela Liddell — who could all confirm that, at seven thirty that same morning, the commandant was being driven to London in a Home Office car. So, Mr Cotter arrived at his office at seven thirty, as usual. He didn't even have time to sit down before his desk phone rang. That call was traced to the phone in Angela's room, and I'm sure it was made by Mrs Dumble, probably as soon as Chaytor-Gill and Miss Liddell left the building. We'll still have to work on this, but it should be easy to prove. As deputy commandant, she'll have had an excuse to call him urgently on some security matter. When he got to the room, she could have been pretending to take a nip of whisky and persuaded him to take a swig — cold day and all that — and he'd be flattered to be sharing a drink with an attractive woman — Felicity could turn on the charm, believe me. All she had to do then was hide the whisky-cyanide bottle in a drawer with Angela's underwear and get out of there fast. She would know she had to have the whole thing done by between seven thirty and about seven fifty, when Angela usually got back from her run."

Blade took a breath. "Yesterday, I obtained two search warrants, and today launched 'Operation Bramshill,' a raid on the suites occupied by Chaytor-Gill and Mrs Dumble, led by DCs Headley and Robinson, accompanied by several computer experts. So, DC Headley, would you continue?"

Bill cleared his throat. "There was no one home, so we forced the doors. I entered Mr Chaytor-Gill's apartment and DC Robinson Mrs Dumble's. We each had two computer experts with us. And we both struck gold. Mr Chaytor-Gill's computer revealed he had paid for, and received, cyanide from an American source."

"And Mrs Dumble had been trying to find recipes for cyanide," Tony added. "I also found, in her apartment, a pair of black trousers and an anorak, as well as a truncheon — probably a souvenir from her early days on the beat — and a pair of wellingtons. All have been bagged for forensics, with the attack on PC Harper in mind."

"The commandant also had a black outfit and wellingtons, which we've bagged," said Bill. "The imprints of one of the pair of wellies should be a match for moulds we made from the trail of footprints leading from the window of Inspector Liddell's room. It was false, of course. One of them could have left by the window and then, once on the hard, icy road gone to the front of the block and walked down the corridor in stockinged feet."

"Finally," Tony said, "Mr Chaytor-Gill's mobile has come up trumps. The number of the camera in the hall is in the phone's gallery — it's even labelled 'Hall' — and I'm sure the experts will be able to discover the date and times it was snapped."

Chief Constable Bainbridge was smiling broadly. "Well done, all of you," he boomed. He shook Blade's hand, adding, "I knew I could rely on you, Ralph. That's one in the eye for the Yard, eh!"

After a few more pleasantries and a handshake from Stan Oliver, they were gone.

After congratulating Bill and Tony on their good work, Blade sent them home. Slowly, he gathered all his personal items and put them on the desktop. He would send Adrian to pick them up tomorrow.

He struggled into his heavy overcoat — and fought to get at his mobile as, once more, it played *Für Elise*. It was Dorothy to say that the prisoners had been charged, had seen their solicitors and were safely locked up. He told her to have the team assembled at the police station at nine tomorrow morning. Finally, he rang home to say he was on the way.

The light was dying and it was starting to snow as he tramped to the car. He wondered vaguely what would happen at the college, now suddenly minus both a commandant and a deputy. Then he decided he didn't care. That was somebody else's problem. Now, he was more concerned with how things were at home.

Julie had prepared an extra special liver and bacon dinner.

EPILOGUE

ALMOST SEVEN months passed before the case was heard in the Crown Court. Roderick Chaytor-Gill and Felicity Dumble were charged with murder and conspiracy to murder and were found guilty on both counts. Each received two life sentences, with a recommendation that a minimum of thirty years be served.

Keith Dumble and his new wife, Anthea (the former Mrs Chaytor-Gill), didn't wait to hear the sentences. They had left on a delayed honeymoon after staying to give evidence at the trial.

As soon as their spouses had been charged with murder, they had filed for divorce, there no longer being any reason for secrecy. Five months later, they were married. They did keep quiet about that though, to avoid more publicity.

Superintendent Jack Wriggley failed to get Harold Ashington's old job and was told quietly that he would never get further promotion at Scotland Yard. Having served long enough for a full pension he resigned and married Sylvia, who sold her house. The couple plan to live in Mallorca.

On the evening after the sentencing a small, impromptu celebration took place in the Blades' home. The same people were present as on that first evening, almost eight months earlier, when Dorothy, John Hyde and Becky had been welcomed into the fold. This time Bob Fraser was also present, still basking in the glory of his scoop about the arrest of the Bramshill murderers. He had been promoted to the position of editor-at-large at the *Record*, off the diary and free to hunt for unusual stories.

Bob had taken a bottle of whisky to the party, while Dorothy provided her own homemade speciality — corned beef and potato pie. Becky Hyde's offering was a sherry trifle, and John brought a bottle of red wine. It was a warm, early September evening and Julie, aided by her husband, had set out salads and cold meats on the patio table.

Happily, Blade surveyed the people — friends and loved ones — assembled. Everything was going well. His relationships with Julie and Richard — who was currently spending his summer vacation travelling in Asia — were both healing nicely.

His wife came to stand beside him. "It's been a good day," she said. "But, tell me, Ralph, what would you have done if you *had* discovered that I was Ashington's killer?"

Blade frowned and thought for a moment, before giving her a small smile. "That is something that no one, me included, will ever know."

He moved across to Dorothy and drew her aside. "I'm sure we're going to become a damned good team — and I really like your Bob. Do you know what? I think, in future operations, we might make him our own undercover cop." Then, seeing his inspector's delighted smile, he added hastily, "Unpaid."

"Ee!" said Dorothy.

THE END

FREE KINDLE BOOKS

Please join our mailing list for free Kindle books
and new releases, including crime thrillers, mysteries,
romance and more!

www.joffebooks.com

Follow us on Facebook, Twitter and Instagram
@joffebooks

DO YOU LOVE FREE AND BARGAIN BOOKS?

Thank you for reading this book. If you enjoyed it
please leave feedback on Amazon, and if there is anything
we missed or you have a question about then please get in
touch. The author and publishing team appreciate your
feedback and time reading this book.

We hate typos too but sometimes they slip through.
Please send any errors you find to
corrections@joffebooks.com.
We'll get them fixed ASAP. We're very grateful to
eagle-eyed readers who take the time to contact us.

Printed in Great Britain
by Amazon